Face the MUSIC

Marianne Levy

MACMILLAN CHILDREN'S BOOKS

First published 2017 by Macmillan Children's Books
an imprint of Pan Macmillan
20 New Wharf Road, London N1 9RR
Associated companies throughout the world
www.panmacmillan.com

ISBN 978-1-5098-0544-0

1 3 5 7 9 8 6 4 2

A CIP catalogue record for this book is available from
the British Library.

Printed and bound by CPI Group (UK) Ltd, Croydon CR0 4YY

To Shelley

So there I was, standing in the wings, ready to do my first major concert. I mean, seriously major, with masses of people watching and goodness knows how many more online.

Even though I'd practised and practised, I was shaking so badly I could barely hold my guitar. My hands were dripping sweat, and there was a fair chance that when I opened my mouth I'd barf all over the stage.

It was no use telling myself that everyone gets nervous. Because this was no ordinary concert.

I was about to sing live to twelve and a half thousand people.

And each and every one of them wanted to kill me.

CHAPTER ONE

Let's rewind.

So basically, I recorded a song in my bedroom. A song called 'Just Me'. I've always written songs, ever since I can remember, and sat in my bedroom and sung them. Like using up all the hot water and leaving my homework on the bus, writing songs is just something that I do. And this song wasn't especially different from the others.

Except that my friend Jaz put it on YouTube.

And it went a bit viral.

OK, a lot viral.

It started with everyone at school and then went sort of crazy. Like, being-played-on-Radio-1-level crazy. Lacey said that her aunt went to Thailand and 'Just Me' was coming out of the speakers there. It's kind of upsetting that my song gets to go to Thailand when I've never managed to get any further than Plymouth.

Anyway, I ended up getting signed to a record label called Top Music, which I still can't really believe, because this is me we're talking about. Katie Cox, pizza lover, boy band hater and possessor of the World's Wonkiest Fringe.

Being signed to Top Music meant all sorts of things. It meant I had my song go to number two in the charts. It meant that I was supposed to be writing music for a concert and an album. And it meant that I was with the same record label as the annoying boy band Karamel.

This last point wasn't particularly significant, except that, in a moment of extreme foolishness, I'd promised my classmate Savannah that I would get her tickets to go and see them, and she would not let me forget it. Seriously, the girl was obsessed.

'Katie, you know those Karamel tickets . . . ?'

and

'You did promise me, Katie.'

and

'It's, like, completely fine and everything but they are touring at the moment and you made me a promise and if you don't keep it I will tell the entire internet about the time at my birthday party when you fell into my cake. I have pictures, Katie.'

We were at school, sitting in the scrubby bit behind the back of the labs. You'd think that a number-two-selling pop star would, perhaps, have

 4

more glamorous places to be.

In fact, a month on and I hadn't seen any money from my mega hit, and even if it did ever turn up, Mum assured me that there was no way I was allowed to spend it on starting a new life in Hollywood. And, actually, for all my pleading, I wasn't entirely sure I wanted to live alone in a mansion made of gold. At least not until after the end-of-term disco.

'All right, FINE,' I said.

'Really?' Savannah's face was shining like I'd opened up her head and stuck a tea light in her mouth. 'Babes, you are rocking my world. Backstage passes, yes, yes?'

You would also think that being a number-two-selling pop star would elevate me into a position at least slightly above Savannah, even if she was the richest and prettiest girl in my form.

Oh well.

I started texting the head of Top Music. 'I'm asking.'

> Hi Tony, I was wondering if my friend could have a ticket and backstage pass to see Karamel when they come to London? Thanks, Katie.

 5

'OK?' I held it up to show her.

'Eew!' said Savannah, who has seen far too many American high school movies. 'You cannot seriously expect me to go on my own.'

'I seriously can.'

At which point Savannah went grey, which is quite hard to do when you're slathered in spray tan. 'Katie. You are asking me to meet my future boyfriend while looking . . .' She paused, her mouth making funny little shapes as she tried to bend her lips around the word 'unpopular'.

Now, there is a big difference between looking unpopular and being unpopular and, unlike Savannah, I have experienced both. So even though, really, I think Savannah would probably benefit from a dose of unpopularity, I softened enough to say:

'All right. I'll ask for two tickets.'

Sofie and Paige pinged upright, and Savannah's head swivelled from one to the other. In the space of ten seconds she'd gone from wounded possum to queen cobra.

'Pleeeease can I come?' said Sofie. 'I will give you anything you want, Savannah.'

'I'll give you double,' said Paige. 'My fake Gucci purse, even. Anything.'

'But that's not fair!' cried Sofie. 'I don't have a fake Gucci purse to give!'

I am not one to mess with a friendship as beautiful as the Sofie-Savannah-Paige triangle, although I have to say, I did consider it. But the fallout would have been too great, both for the world and its fake Gucci leatherwear.

'Three tickets,' I said. 'I will ask for three tickets.'

'Thanks, Katie.'

'Thank you!'

'Can you make it four?'

Now, this was a surprise.

Because the words had come from my best friend, Lacey.

Lacey, who had always agreed with me that boy bands are an insult to music. And that the worst and most insulting boy band of all is Karamel.

'Ha ha ha,' I said. 'You're funny, Lace.'

She wasn't laughing back. 'Yes or no?'

'Lacey, you cannot actually be suggesting that you want to spend an evening watching Karamel.'

'It's either that or watch telly with Mum,' said Lacey,

 7

who, to be fair, does have quite a scary mum.

'But—'

'I want to go,' said Lacey. 'It'll be fun.'

'Four tickets,' I said. And then I hit send.

'Aren't you coming?' said Lacey.

'I am not,' I said. 'On account of Karamel being literally the worst boy band in the whole universe. Also, I have tons of other things to do. I am so busy right now.'

'Whoah, have you *still* not written your song?' said Lacey. 'What's the hold-up?'

'There's no hold-up. It's going great,' I said quickly, and then looked hard at my phone until everyone started talking about something else.

This is the difficulty with having a song do well on the internet. It starts out all exciting and brilliant and everyone says well done and sends the link to their cousin in Australia and maybe you even get a record deal and end up on the front page of the *Harltree Gazette*.

And then, just as you're getting used to everything being sort of awesome, it happens. Someone says:

'So, what's next?'

And once one person's said it, they all do. It's not enough that there's a song out there, a song you're really proud of, that everyone's been clicking on and singing at you in newsagents. Nope.

They want more.

Have you written the next one yet?

When's it out?

We can't wait!

In fact, I had some potential next ones. More than some; loads and loads. Hundreds, really, because I've been writing songs since I was tiny.

Only, somehow, even though I had notebook after notebook full of lyrics, most of them didn't seem quite right. For example, last night I found one I'd started a while back, about spaghetti hoops, and in my memory it was really funny. But when I sat down and actually sang it, it was just this weird unfinished thing about spaghetti hoops. I mean, spaghetti hoops are nice, and all, but I'm not sure they merit their own song.

I still had plenty of decent ones to play Tony, though. And, as I said to myself, over and over and over again, it's only natural to have the jitters – absolutely nothing to worry about.

'Actually,' I said, interrupting a conversation about Karamel's latest album artwork, 'I'm going into Top Music tomorrow to play them some stuff. And I'm sort of feeling a bit anxious about it.'

'I'm not surprised,' said Lacey. 'If I were you I'd be really worried.'

'Would you?' This seemed remarkably insensitive, coming from my BF. 'Huh.'

'Why isn't he replying?' said Savannah, who was more interested in my phone than my creative process. 'Didn't you make it clear that this is important?'

'Savannah, I texted the head of one of the country's biggest music labels. I'm not sure that arranging your concert tickets is right up there on his list of priorities.'

'So you *didn't* make it clear that it was important. Honestly, Katie, becoming a celebrity has made you so self-centred.'

My phone flashed.

Everyone leaned in, Savannah's fingers doing this sort of grabby motion, like one of those claw machines you get at the seaside that always pick up the teddy and then drop it at the very last second, making you spend your entire allowance on a stuffed toy you don't even want when you actually needed the money for fish and chips.

'It's a yes,' I said. 'Next Thursday, four front-row VIP

tickets will be waiting at the box office, plus wristbands for the backstage party afterwards. All sorted, any problems just speak to security. Oh. Next Thursday is July the ninth. That's—'

I stopped talking because the screaming had got so loud and so high that no one would have heard me. It was like someone had stomped on a box of bats.

'Oh my God, I am going to meet Karamel!'

'They are so beautiful!'

'This is it. This is the best thing to ever happen to me.'

'I am going to marry him. This is where it begins. Me and Kurt. Forever!'

'No, *I'm* going to marry him.'

'No, I am.'

The squeaks paused for the tiniest second, and I opened my mouth.

'Can we all just calm down a minute here and—'

At which point Savannah said, 'WHAT AM I GOING TO WEAR?'

And after that I could have said anything at all, to be honest, because no one would have heard me.

So I tried to meet Lacey's eye, with my *Wow, these three are being crazy right now* face.

Only, she wasn't looking at me. She was looking at Paige, and saying:

'Do you think Kristian will talk to me? We could double-date . . .'

And I did wonder whether me and my best friend were ever so slightly growing apart.

Just a bit.

'Katie, babes, are you OK? Because you are making the most ugly face right now.'

'Thanks for letting me know, Savannah.'

'No problem.'

'Actually,' I went on, 'I am a bit upset. Because July the ninth is—'

Only, the bell was ringing, and Savannah and Paige and Sofie and Lacey were swinging off across the car park, chanting 'WE'RE GOING TO SEE KARAMEL' at the top of their voices.

I sighed, and said, 'July the ninth is my birthday.'

But they were too far away to hear.

Spaghetti Hoops

They're orange
And they float in soups
They're pasta
And they're shaped like hoops

Something something spaghetti

Something something

Confetti

Yeti

no

argh!

CHAPTER TWO

'Hang on,' said my big sister Amanda, who had been scrolling through the latest celeb gossip on Pop Trash, but now put her phone down in order to gape at my stupidity. 'You offered half your form free tickets and backstage passes to see the biggest boy band on the planet, and you're upset because they said yes?'

Mands has a very annoying way of seeing things, sometimes.

'They should know better,' I said. 'Well, not Savannah's lot. But Lacey should.'

'Why?'

Honestly. 'Because LACEY HATES KARAMEL.'

Amanda raised one of her eyebrows. 'Does she? Or do you?'

And then she did the big-sister thing she does where she attempts to look really, really wise.

I couldn't even tell her to go back to her own room. Back in the spring Mum and her new boyfriend Adrian had teamed up to buy the world's most useless house and we'd all moved in together.

You wouldn't think that a house *could* be useless, as all it really needs to do is to stand there without falling down. But our house wasn't even managing to do that. There were cracks in the walls and the garage roof had collapsed and when they finally got a surveyor to come round he said that one side of the house had subsidence and needed underpinning as a matter of urgency.

Which is a fancy way of saying that it might fall down.

So now the half of the house with the most cracks in it was strictly out of bounds. Which meant that Amanda's room was out of action. Which meant that she'd had to move in with me.

I'd been trying to look on the bright side of things. It was much easier to borrow her stuff when it was sitting in the same wardrobe as mine.

And . . . Actually, that was pretty much the only positive.

I mean, she's my sister and everything, but is it really necessary for her to fold her pants? Or to make my bed? Or to make me listen to every last track released by Friends of Noom or the Zits or whatever weird and unknown band she's currently into?

'We both hate Karamel,' I told her. 'Boy band? More

 15

like boy bland.' I waited for some acknowledgement of what had been quite a clever thing to say, but Amanda's face wasn't moving, so I carried on. 'Lacey and I have always been extremely clear on the matter. They are the three most annoying boys on the face of the earth and they have stupid hair. Their names all begin with a K. Even Kolin. I mean, come on. Kolin! And they can't sing.'

'Kurt is a very accomplished singer and a terrific guitarist,' said Mands. 'How much Karamel have you actually heard?'

'I try not to listen to them!' Now I was really getting quite worked up.

'So you agree that you could be wrong?'

By this time I was seriously considering taking up residence in Amanda's old room. Yeah, there was every chance it would crumble and kill me, but if I stayed in the presence of my older sister for very much longer then I was going to kill her.

'I think I might go out for a bit,' I said.

'Don't you have a history essay to do?' said Ms Annoying. 'And a song to write?'

'Yeah, well,' I said.

'And aren't you going in to see Top Music *tomorrow*?'

'Yes. And . . .'

'Katie, do you have anything to play them? Anything at all?'

'There's a song about spaghetti hoops,' I said. 'It's . . . it's not very good.' I threw myself face down on to my bed, which had a bowl of cornflake mush on the pillow, which I didn't notice until it had gone everywhere. 'Uuuurgh.'

'Well, if you will leave food there . . .'

'I can't write, Manda. I've forgotten how to do it! I sit down and I stare at the page and nothing seems to come out and I don't understand. And now I have cereal gunge in my nostrils.'

She got down on her haunches beside me, and handed me a T-shirt to mop up the mess. And actually, when I looked up and saw her expression of genuine concern, I felt a proper little shiver of fear.

'Katie, of course you know how to do it. You just need to start believing in yourself again.'

'I do believe in myself! I know I can write songs. What I don't know is why I can't seem to write them *at the moment*.'

'Uh,' said Amanda, which seemed to sum it up.

'I'm going out for some fresh air,' I said.

 17

So out I went, off down the lane, doing my usual pause at the corner before the bus stop in case my fellow classmate and all-round nutcase Mad Jaz was there. Not that I was avoiding her or anything; it's just useful to have a bit of a warning before you see Mad Jaz, because of her being so mad.

Like, a few months ago, this young teaching assistant guy gave her a telling-off for wearing non-regulation tights. No one knows how she did it, but the next day when he came into school, all his hair had fallen out. Even his eyebrows.

Or how she's apparently been banned from every single branch of Lidl. Not just in Harltree. Not even just in Essex. She's been banned from every branch in the WORLD.

The bus stop appeared. And, phew. She wasn't there.

I carried on, down towards the main road, half thinking I should go back. That's the problem with walks. You have to have a plan before you set off or they feel a bit pointless.

Then my phone started to go.

It was Dad.

I answered on the third ring.

'Dad! Hi!'

'How's my little superstar?'

'Really well, thanks.'

'House still standing?'

'Of course it is,' I said, because the only thing worse than living in a falling-down house was admitting as much to Dad. When he and Mum divorced we had to sell our old house, and somehow he'd managed to rent a pad in America with his half of the cash, right on the beach, while we ended up in chaos. His flat looked like the kind of place you'd go to on holiday. No – correction. It looked like the kind of place Savannah would go to on holiday. And Savannah gets her jeans from Harrods.

'Great! And how's your new career?'

'Um. Actually, Dad, I could do with a bit of advice on that. I've got this big meeting tomorrow with the record label and I'm supposed to play them a load of new stuff. Only, I haven't written any.'

When I said it out loud, it sounded very, very bad.

'Easy! Just play them some of your old stuff and tell them it's new. They won't know the difference.'

'But . . . I played lots of it at the concert in Adrian's shop.'

'Like anyone remembers exactly what you played.'

It wasn't the best solution, but it was *a* solution. 'OK, maybe I'll try that.'

'How is Mr Scuzzy Record Shop?'

'Adrian? He's really well, thanks. And the shop's so busy. You know Mands is working in there full time now, and she's doing this gig night once a week, with new bands, it's been selling out.' There was this pause and I was clearly supposed to ask him about his new partner too. I lasted as long as I could, which was two seconds, and then I said it: 'And how's Catriona?'

'Not so good,' said Dad.

Which was a first. Ever since he went stateside, Dad's life has been one hundred per cent fantastic.

'Er, how do you mean?' I said. 'She's not ill, is she?' I knew as I said it that she probably wasn't. I mean, Catriona is a twenty-five-year-old vegan Pilates instructor. They don't get ill. They can't.

'She's found a new direction.'

'What direction was she going in before?'

'Katie, Catriona and I have decided to uncouple.'

Ah.

'Oh Dad, I'm sorry,' I said, which wasn't necessarily

true, but he seemed glad I'd said it.

'Probably for the best,' said Dad. 'Because of the apartment.'

'Still seeing dolphins from the kitchen window?' I asked.

'Yes. No.' He cleared his throat. This was turning out to be the strangest Dad conversation ever. 'The dolphins haven't gone anywhere. But I have.'

'But why?'

'Fancied a change, didn't I? A man can have too many dolphins.'

'So, where are you living now?'

'Well,' said Dad. 'Thought I might head over to see you guys for a bit. While I'm between places.'

'Seriously?' I thought my heart might tear out of my chest and explode. 'That would be brilliant! When were you thinking? Next month? Or is that too soon? Sorry, that's probably too soon, isn't it?'

'I can't wait until next month to see my best girl. How about . . . next week?'

'Next week? Wow. Yes. YES!'

'Hold on . . .' There was a pause and some tapping. 'Confirmed. Sorry, I was just buying the plane ticket.'

'BRILLIANT! Will you bring your guitar?'

'Sure thing-a-ling.'

'I can't wait,' I said, because I couldn't.

'Got to go, Katie. But – can I ask a quick favour?'

'Anything.'

'Could you tell your mother for me?'

'Sure,' I said.

'Love you, K.'

'Love you too, Dad. I'm so glad you're coming home.'

Well, after that I was practically dancing. I know this because three cars on the main road slowed down to honk at me.

So I swung back up towards our lane, noticing how the air smelt better and the sky was just that bit more blue.

And perhaps I should have spent a little more time looking at what was going on straight ahead rather than sniffing the breeze and tilting my head at the clouds. Because I neglected to do my usual around-the-corner check and ran smack bang into Mad Jaz.

She was wearing this top that was half red netting and half slashed black shiny stuff, along with a truly epic level of liquid eyeliner.

I did consider pretending that I hadn't seen her and carrying on walking, but I decided against it. Jaz and I are sort of friends these days, although it's a slightly uneasy friendship, at least from my side of things, as it's based partly on liking Jaz, but also partly on fear.

Also, Jaz had seen me and was calling, 'Katie!'

'Hi, Jaz,' I said.

'How's the songwriting?' said Jaz.

'Oh, you know,' I mumbled. Then, to change the subject to something that I actually wanted to talk about, 'My dad's coming home. From America! Maybe he'll be back for my birthday? He said next week, and my birthday's on Thursday . . .'

'I thought your dad was that guy you live with.'

'Adrian? Urgh, no! Adrian is Mum's boyfriend. No. My dad's this super-cool musician who lives in California. And he's coming back next week.'

'OK,' said Jaz.

'So I can't stay and chat,' I said. 'I have to go home and tell Mum.'

'Why are *you* telling her?'

'He asked me if I would.'

'So he's laid it on you? Nice of him.'

'It was, actually,' I said. 'Dad wanted me to know first. We have this really special relationship. And anyway, Mum will be fine with it; she's got Adrian now.'

Jaz fell into step beside me. 'Has he always been in America?'

'No,' I said, speeding up in the hope that maybe she'd drop back and go away. She didn't. 'He moved there a few months ago, after the divorce. He got this cool flat by the sea. You can watch dolphins from the kitchen window. Well, you could. He's just moved out.' Then, as I thought about it properly, 'Maybe there's a chance that he's back forever. How cool would that be?!'

'Depends,' said Jaz. 'Was it one of those good divorces, where everyone stays friends?'

I really wanted to say yes. But I couldn't. It had pretty much been the opposite of that. 'Not especially,' I said.

'And your mum thought he was safely in America. Only now he's back in just a few days, and he wasn't even brave enough to tell her himself, so he's got you doing it,' said Jaz.

'That is a very twisted way of looking at things,' I told her. Although I have to say, the sky had gone back to its normal colour and I could definitely detect a bit of diesel on the breeze.

We'd reached my front door.

'Good luck,' said Jaz.

'What for?'

Jaz smiled. 'Katie, you are about to tell your mum that your dad, who she hates, is coming home next week, and that he was too cowardly to tell her himself.'

'Honestly, Jaz. It's no big deal. See you Monday, OK?'

And then I was back in the hall, with its familiar smell of damp and a strange sort of soupiness that we'd recently traced to a particular patch of carpet.

I couldn't go upstairs, not with You Know Who in *my* bedroom. So I went into the kitchen, instead.

'Katie, love!'

'Oh, hi, Mum.'

'Are you all right? Has something happened?'

I was going to tell her, I really was. It's just, I don't know, maybe Mad Jaz had spooked me with her madness.

'No,' I said. 'Nothing's happened.'

'In that case, why haven't you done the washing-up?'

'Because,' I said, trying to keep the wobble out of my voice, 'I have a very important meeting with my record label tomorrow, and I am TRYING to write a song.'

CHAPTER THREE

I think it's fair to say that as far as my music career is concerned, Mum is not a fan.

This is for a number of reasons. Some of them are fair enough. Others are completely nuts.

- And I do appreciate that this is a big one – Tony, the head of my record label, had sort of tried to destroy my entire life in order to get revenge on Mum's new boyfriend, Adrian. So yes, all right, I can see why she might have a few trust issues when it comes to Top Music. I kind of have them too, even though ever since my single went into the charts they have been very nice indeed, sending me chocolates and cards and more bunches of flowers than we have vases to put them in (i.e. two).
- Mum reckons that it will stop me from putting any effort into my schoolwork. I pointed out to her that I never put much effort into my schoolwork anyway. This did not seem to help.

- Dad is a musician. This means that I am not allowed to be a musician too. No, I don't understand this one either.

After the whole single-going-viral-concert thing had happened, Tony took Mum and Adrian and Manda and me out for dinner in London at this ultra-glam restaurant called The Ivy. Me and Mands spent most of the meal celebrity-spotting (we saw Amanda Holden, Stephen Fry and someone who we are fairly sure is in *Game of Thrones*), while the adults talked about contracts and percentages and things that I did want to be interested in, but somehow found I wasn't.

By the end, and after a couple of glasses of champagne, Mum was smiling, and even let Tony kiss her on both cheeks, although once he'd got into the back of his fancy black car outside, she said, 'I don't trust that man as far as I can throw him.' But it seemed that she had agreed to 'see how things go', which, when I quizzed Adrian later, meant she would let me record an album, so long as I didn't take even a single morning off school and that any money I made was put into an account that I couldn't get to until I was about seventy.

 27

'And the second it makes you unhappy, then that's it, game over,' said Adrian.

'Of course,' I said.

So on the morning of going in to see Top Music, I made sure to seem especially upbeat, singing in the shower and eating three of the four slightly stale croissants Adrian had found reduced in Morrisons.

'I still don't know, Katie,' said Mum, looking down at a sea of pastry flakes. 'I just think—'

'I *know* what you just think,' I told her. 'And I'm just saying, let me try it. If I don't like it, I'll stop.'

We'd already had this conversation about seventeen times in the last week. I really couldn't see why we needed to be having it again now, when there was a train to catch and people waiting for me.

Which I told her. And she sighed.

'It's going to change you, Katie.'

'Er, I don't think so.'

'Well, what if it changes the people around you? How are you going to feel when your friends start treating you differently? Some people are weak, Katie, and who knows what they'll do for a bit of attention, an envelope full of cash . . .'

'Like who? Lacey?'

'I don't want to see you hurt,' said Mum. 'That's all.'

'I know,' I said. 'But I won't be. Adrian'll look after me. You trust *him*, don't you?'

I said this knowing full well that Mum would not be able to say that, no, she didn't trust her boyfriend. And then, as I'd hoped, she gave me a kiss and headed off to the hospital for her shift, leaving me to exchange a look with Adrian, and swipe the final croissant.

'Katie, hello! And Adrian! Mate! So great to see you both.'

And then there we were in Top Music's great big glass meeting room – me, my guitar and Adrian.

That was our side of the table. In the middle there was a plate of (what I knew from past experience would be really delicious) biscuits. Then on the other side sat Tony Topper, the head of Top Music, with his rich-man stubble and bright white teeth, and skin that would make an orange feel pale.

'So, we're just finalizing the details for your first concert,' said Tony.

'Er, OK. Um.'

He leaned forward and I wondered how he made his

shirt so incredibly crisp. Maybe he just got a new one out of the packet every morning. That's what I'd do.

'You seem a bit worried.'

'Well, yes. I've never done a big concert before. I mean, the only one I've done was in the shop, which is tiny and in Harltree and full of mouldy old vinyl.' I remembered the shop's owner was sitting next to me. 'But you know, completely supercool.'

'It's OK, Katie,' murmured Adrian.

'All I'm saying is that . . . I'm a tiny bit worried about it,' I said. 'Not, you know, super worried. Just, averagely worried. The normal level of worried.'

Tony showed me a mouthful of expensive teeth.

'No problem, Katie. We'll keep this first one pretty small, shall we? More of a showcase than a concert. Intimate and low key. Just have some industry people in, a select group of fans, a few friends, and that's it.' He took a sip of coffee. 'And of course put the word out that you're playing and then make sure no one can get tickets. That's always a good way to generate buzz for a new artist. Get you trending on social media.'

I'm sorry, but there is literally nothing more cringey

than when a grown-up says 'trending on social media'. Tony may be a humongously successful music boss with all the world's money, but 'trending on social media'? Er, I don't think so.

'And if it all goes well, we'll have you playing Wembley soon enough. So –' he nodded towards my guitar – 'shall we?'

At which point I kind of got a bit panicky and spent far too long tuning up, during which Adrian ate two biscuits and got crumbs all over the table.

'OK,' I said, eventually, when I couldn't put it off any longer. 'So, this is "Cake Boyfriend", which is kind of my favourite song from everything I have. I mean, it's maybe not quite single material. But I think it should definitely be on the album. Maybe.'

And then I started to play.

Now, here's the thing. I wasn't at all feeling it when I started.

But music's sort of like magic, isn't it? Not that I believe in magic, but if I did, I'd say that songs are spells, and as you're singing them, you're kind of pulling everyone around you into this glimmery bubble where nothing else matters. It's just you and the music.

The song finished, and I stopped, and smiled, feeling a bit giddy.

And Tony said, 'That's fine, I suppose. Anything else?'

Then I played through 'Song for a Broken Phone', only Tony said that most people get free upgrades on their contracts and are quite glad when their phones break as it gives them an excuse to get a new one.

So I played 'London Yeah', only Tony said that it was too UK-focused, and I needed to think about foreign audiences, and so I sort of gave up and concentrated on eating the remaining biscuits, which in fact weren't quite as nice as I'd remembered.

'Katie, forgive me if I'm wrong,' said Tony, who did not look like a man who thought he was wrong, or who thought he needed to be forgiven, 'but didn't you play all these songs at the record-shop concert?'

Rumbled. 'Maybe . . .'

'Have you got anything new? Anything at all?'

'I've got the beginnings of a song about spaghetti hoops,' I said.

The awkward pause that followed lasted for something like infinity.

'We'll send over some ideas,' said Tony. 'And it's great

that you're coming to the Karamel gig. Kurt's a real fan of yours.'

'Oh, I'm not actually—'

'You two should collaborate on something.'

'Er.'

'Great, I'll run it by him.' He saw me eyeing what was left of the biscuits. 'Have one, have one! They're here for you. And congratulations again, Katie. We're so excited.'

'Me too.'

'Just, try not to put too much pressure on yourself, OK? With the writing. It'll come.'

'OK,' I said, through a big mouthful of biscuit.

'If you can,' said Tony, 'try to go for something incredibly universal, that'll really translate. Something that your fans can latch on to, like they did with "Just Me". Funny but serious. Introspective but upbeat. You know the kind of thing.'

'Um, yes.'

'We're certain you'll come up with it very soon.'

'Um, yes.'

'I'm sure you're feeling as confident about Katie as I am,' said Adrian, giving my shoulders a squeeze. A couple of months ago this behaviour would have qualified as unacceptable, but now, I must admit I was grateful for it.

Especially when I reached for another biscuit and Tony said:

'About that.'

'The biscuit?'

'Yes. This is a little delicate, Katie. But, you're going to be in the public eye quite a lot, soon. And I'm sure you'll agree that it would be great for you to go into all of this really feeling . . . and looking . . . your best.'

Was Tony calling me fat?

'So if you'd like a personal trainer, or for us to get you on to a meal plan, just let us know. Top Music is here to help.'

He was!

'Thanks,' I said. 'I'll, um, bear that in mind.' I pushed the plate away.

'I've got to get back to it now, conference call to the Glastonbury people. Remember, I'm on the end of my phone, day and night, if you ever want to play me anything.'

'OK.'

'Don't let the pressure get to you,' said Tony. 'The last thing we want is for you to get some kind of creative block.'

I must have looked startled as he coughed.

'Crystal Skye had one, after her first concert. We waited and waited, and eventually we locked her in a hotel room for a week.'

'And then she wrote a new song?' said Adrian.

'No, she had a nervous breakdown!' said Tony, getting to his feet, which meant we had to do the same. 'But *then* she wrote a song. So, it worked!'

CHAPTER FOUR

Jaz is one of those people who seems to take up a lot of room. I'm not saying she's big or anything. In fact, she's a lot thinner than me. It's just, she has this really enormous aura that fills up all the space you put her in, whether it's my bedroom or our form room or, as with right now, the top deck of the bus. I hope we don't ever get stuck in a lift together. I'd probably suffocate.

'You've got a lot of Amy Winehouse stuff,' said Jaz, scrolling through my iTunes, which was a little surprising, because I hadn't given her my phone. The thing was far too precious to ever leave my hand, being new, and nice, and literally the only thing that had come out of all this fame stuff so far.

Also, I'm not massively trusting of Jaz around phones, because of how she managed to film me on hers, put the video online and send me viral, with the result that I nearly lost my best friend, alienated the rest of my form and almost broke up Mum and Adrian.

I reached out and took it back again. How she'd got it

in the first place was beyond me. I made a mental note to keep it behind a zip. Maybe two.

'Amy's music is amazing,' I said, gazing out the window, and then starting backwards as the bus smacked into the branches of an overhanging tree. 'She only did two albums, but every single track is just, you know . . .'

'How's your album going?' said Jaz.

I'd always thought it's best, with people like Jaz, not to ever show any sign of weakness, because they'll just use it against you later. But recently I'd changed my opinion of her. Not that I'd decided she was the world's nicest person or anything, but she had been, well, sort of, kind of, nice.

Which is why I felt like it would be OK to say, 'Not as well as I thought it was.'

We stopped talking for a moment as, two rows ahead, Nicole from year ten lifted up her hair to show the year sevens her infected ear-piercing.

'I don't get it,' said Jaz. 'You've got hundreds of songs. You showed me them. In your book.'

For the record, I hadn't shown her, she'd gone into my bag and found them, but hey-ho.

'Yeah, but the next one's got to be drop-dead incredible

or everyone will say I'm a one-hit wonder and I'll just be this complete has-been for the entire rest of my life. And with "Just Me", it was like I wrote it without even thinking about it, and it somehow came out all right. But now the more I think about it, the less I can do anything. It's like, everything that happens to me, I'm saying, "Is that a song?" and so it never is.'

'Why can't you use one of the ones you already have?'

'Tony didn't like any of them.' It was the first time I'd said it out loud. 'We had this big meeting and I played him loads of stuff and he kept saying it didn't work.'

'Even "Cake Boyfriend"?'

'Even "Cake Boyfriend". And then when I got home I had this email. Hold on . . .' I found it and showed her, being sure to keep my fingers firmly wrapped around the screen.

Katie!

Great meeting.

Loved revisiting your back catalogue! You are such a talent.

Our feeling is that you should try to write a brand-new single.

Possible themes:

• A song about partying. Please, no references to anything inappropriate.

• A song about first love. Please, no references to anything inappropriate.

• Something about animals. Maybe cats? People on social media love cats. Do you have a cat? If not, we can lend you one.

Hope that's got you feeling inspired! If you want to run any ideas by me, my door is always open!

Looking forward to hearing from you.

Tony

'So he wants a song about going to a party where you fall in love with a cat,' said Jaz.

'Yeah.'

'I wouldn't mind hearing that,' said Jaz, unhelpfully.

'Don't hold your breath,' I said, wondering if I felt a bit sick because of our conversation, or just from reading a screen while sitting on the top deck of a bus. 'I'll have to come up with something soon, but I don't know what it'll be.' Then, 'Sorry, are you OK there?'

I was starting to suspect Jaz wasn't completely focused on what I was saying, on account of how she had my phone (again?! How???) and was frantically typing.

'JAZ!'

'It's all right. I'm not logged in as you.'

'Can't you use yours?'

'I'm out of data.'

I looked to check she really wasn't logged in as me, because that really would have been a major disaster, and then said:

'What are you doing?'

'Giving Nicole's troll the smackdown.'

'Nicole has a troll?'

'Yeah,' said Jaz, her fingers a blur. 'Every time she posts a video he pops up from his troll hole and tells her she's rank.'

'What's she been posting?'

'How she had her wart frozen off.' Jaz finished whatever she was typing and chucked my phone back into my lap.

I picked it up and had a look. There was Nicole's

video, paused on a picture of her elbow, which I decided I wouldn't examine too carefully.

Then, underneath, a load of likes, a few thumbs down, and people like Devi and Fin and Paige saying things like 'URGH!' and 'way cool, Nicole,' and 'so gross I luv it'. Followed by approximately a hundred and twenty posts, all from someone calling themselves sampand45xcg1, saying:

Harltree scum

and

THE WORLD DOES NOT NEED YOU

and

u r a disgusting cow

And so on, and on, and on.

It was kind of upsetting. And I say that as someone who finds Nicole a tiny bit disgusting, too.

Jaz picked at the lace on her scarf as I tried to imagine

 41

what it would be like to be on the receiving end of something so grim. Tried, and failed. In the end, I decided I would never put anything out there that would get anyone quite so worked up.

'It's weird that they've latched on to Nicole,' I said. 'Maybe she should just stop posting stuff. Or ignore them. It's just words; it's not like it matters.'

Jaz gave me a 'Jaz' look, which reminded me that Jaz is really quite scary sometimes, and that even though she and I were on fairly good terms at the moment it was probably better if I carried on being a little bit careful in her company.

It also made me think that any troll who dared take her on would be a total idiot, because while a troll is a troll, Jaz is Jaz.

Meanwhile, IRL, Nicole was squirting white gunge out of her ear and Finlay was burping up his breakfast and trying to make us guess what he'd eaten, which made me feel sicker than ever.

So I shut my eyes and lay back, and tried, and failed to think of a song.

CHAPTER FIVE

Take it from me, you don't want to be doing English homework and simultaneously trying to write a world-conquering hit single. Unless, maybe, the hit single is about English homework, but I sent the idea to Tony and got a single-word reply. A word that began with an 'n' and ended with an 'o'.

Still, at least I had my best friend to turn to for support.

'I am so stressed right now,' I said.

We were digesting a particularly grim school lunch, I'd just finished a guitar lesson, and we were sitting on the radiators along the top corridor. It's nice up there. The radiators mean it's warm even in winter, and there's a really good view. Only of the car park, but still, a car park is better than a brick wall. Which is about as much as you can see from the lower corridor, where we'd sat in year seven.

It was sad that I knew without even having to ask that Tony wouldn't let me release a song about corridors.

'What's there to be stressed about?' said Lacey, who

was rocking a particularly breezy look. She'd clipped her fringe back and rolled down her sock to display the bronze ankle bracelet we'd found on our last trip to Oxfam. 'Mellow down. It's summer, babes.'

'*Babes?*' I repeated. '"Babes" is a Savannah word.'

'Well, anyway, it's summer,' said Lacey. 'Which is the least stressful time of year.'

'Unless you have heat rash.'

'I don't get heat rash.'

'Or chafing,' I said.

'I told you, stick some talc in there.'

'And exams.'

'I'm not thinking about that.'

'Then what about wasps, Lacey? I can just about maybe believe you're not as sweaty as I am, and that maybe your epic-level exam denial is keeping you from freaking out, but you have an extreme phobia of wasps!'

'I'm over it.'

This did not seem likely, as, last year at sports day, Lacey got chased by a wasp in the 400 metres and set a new school record. Which was quite something, given that she wasn't even in the race.

'I thought we were all about winter,' I said. 'You know.

With the Christmas carols and pies. And big coats!'

'Savannah says I've got a great back,' said Lacey. 'You can't show off your back in a big coat.'

I took a moment to consider Lacey's back. From what I could remember, it was just a normal back. Which I told her.

'Actually,' said Lacey, looking a bit offended, 'Sav says it's way better than average. I don't have spots, or back fat, and my shoulders are this perfect ratio to the rest of me. I'm thinking I might go backless to the disco. Show it off a bit.'

'Right.'

'Katie, are you being unsupportive of my back?'

'No. I love your back. I'm its biggest fan. Second biggest, after Savannah.'

'Good.'

There was a silence. 'We've got so much work at the moment,' I said. 'I just feel like however much I do, I ought to be doing more.'

'Then why aren't you working now?' Lacey wanted to know. 'You could go to the library.'

Which wasn't the point. 'It's the *idea* of working that I find so hard. It's all this invisible pressure.'

 45

'Seriously,' said Lacey. 'If you want to go, I won't stop you.'

'Plus, I can't seem to think of a new song. I just spent a whole entire guitar lesson with Jill trying to come up with something and nothing happened and nothing happened and then I finally had this idea but when I tried it out Jill said I was playing the verses of "Don't Stop Believin'" and the chorus of "Empire State of Mind".'

Was it my imagination, or did Lacey very slightly roll her eyes?

It was my imagination. Of course it was. Because then she said:

'Let's write one now. We could call it . . . "By the Radiators".'

'Er, no.'

'"Looking Down into the Car Park"?'

'Lace, it's OK; no one wants you to write it for me,' I said. And for some reason I couldn't even begin to understand, she twitched, and looked away.

I searched around my brain for things to cheer us both up a bit. Usually, the inside of my head is like my bedroom floor, filled with interesting items if you can just find them underneath all the junk. Today, though, there was pretty much nothing.

Nothing except for Dad.

Ever since the phone call, the word had been going around my head like a drumbeat.

Dad.

Dad.

Dad.

Dad.

And – well, you get it.

I was desperate to tell Lacey, crazy keen to talk about it with someone who'd understand. Not Mands. She'd been down on Dad ever since he went to America, even though he'd had no choice, because work is work, plus, America is awesome.

And telling Mum . . . well, to be completely honest, I was still working up to that.

But my best friend would understand, wouldn't she? Lacey knew the whole entire history of the divorce. She'd even been lucky enough to witness a couple of the rows.

Which is, I suppose, what had stopped me from saying anything so far. Lace completely got it, of course she did, but if there was even a chance that she'd be anything less than totally excited for me, then it wasn't a conversation

I was particularly interested in having.

But she would be. Of course she would be. She'd met him. And now she'd be seeing him again. Maybe he'd even take us out for dinner . . .

'Dad's coming home,' I said, just as Lacey said:

'Savannah's dad's hiring a pink stretch limo to take us to the Karamel concert.'

'What? That is so tacky.' Perhaps it was better to leave the family stuff for the moment.

'. . . Yeah. And we're getting majorly dressed up first, at Paige's house.'

'What a hassle.'

A group of boys from our year came past. A group that included Dominic Preston, who is extremely good-looking.

He gave me a smile and I fell off the radiator.

'Keep walking please, nothing to see here,' said Lacey, picking me up from the floor.

He laughed, and carried on down the corridor.

'Now that *is* an above-average back,' I said, dusting off various bits of top corridor scuzz that had stuck themselves to my skirt.

'Katie!' said Lacey. 'Are you in love with Dominic

Preston? Whoah, are you going to ask him to the disco?'

'He is extremely good-looking,' I admitted.

'I thought we'd agreed to fall in love at the same time so that we could talk about it together.'

We had agreed this, when we were eleven, and falling in love had been as academic as something that was actually academic, like trigonometry. I think we'd even pinkie promised, which is embarrassing, partly because I don't like to break that kind of thing, and also, pinkie promises are extremely whack.

'I cannot control my heart,' I told Lacey.

'So you ARE in love with him! That is SO unfair! Who am I supposed to fall in love with?'

'You're basically in love with Savannah,' I mumbled.

'What?'

'I don't know. Um, Devi Lester? Finlay? You could totally go to the disco with Finlay.'

'Finlay smells of pickled onion Monster Munch.'

'And do you find that attractive in a guy?'

'NO!'

I did, for a second, wonder what it was that I found attractive in Dominic Preston, and whether I really was in love with him. There was his extremely good-looking face, of course, a sort of biggish nose, and grey-blue eyes. And his mouth was the right size for a mouth. Not small, like Finlay's, with his little nibbly rabbit teeth. And not huge and flappy, like Devi Lester's. Kissing Devi Lester would be genuinely hazardous. He'd probably get most of your face in there. You'd be at risk of losing your chin.

Kissing Dominic Preston, though . . . What would that be like? He was a smiley sort of a person, so it would maybe be quite fun. Probably he'd make a joke and then I'd laugh and he'd smile.

Having him get properly close, though . . . maybe even sticking his tongue in my mouth . . . hmm. I probably did want him to, but not anything like as much as, say, wanting the green suede slingbacks I'd seen last week in River Island.

Because . . . unlike the slingbacks, which were definitely amazing, kissing Dominic Preston might be, well, a bit yucky. Not having kissed anyone before, it was hard to know what to expect. And when it comes to kissing, there are so many things to worry about.

Supposing it turns out that he doesn't ever clean his teeth? Supposing he leans in and I find that I have to be sick and I'm trapped in the kiss and I end up heaving into his open mouth???

I mean, I've never heard of it happening before, but there's a first time for everything.

A rush of year sevens told us that it wasn't ever so long before the end of lunch, and we gathered up our stuff.

And Lacey said, in the most casual possible way, so casual that she made sure to look at her bag rather than me, 'You sure you don't want to come to Karamel with us?'

'You're deigning to invite me to come to something that you're only going to because I gave you tickets in the first place?'

'Huh?'

'I mean, how can *you* invite *me*, when the whole thing was my idea? That's just . . . wrong.'

The bell rang, and I followed her down the stairs.

'It's just, I know what you'll be like,' said Lacey.

'What's that supposed to mean?'

'You'll go into one of your grumps and sit around in your room and listen to something angry like Utopia—'

'Nirvana.'

'Yeah, them. And you'll be all stroppy and not answer your phone and spend the next week giving me these looks.'

We stopped outside our form room.

'I do not recognize the person you are talking about,' I said. 'If you want to waste a perfectly good evening watching the World's Worst Band, then fine. But I have other things to do. I mean, boy band? Boy bland, more like.'

'See?' She turned around headed for her desk. 'You're doing it already!'

And before I could reply, Sofie and Paige came floating over in a cloud of Vera Wang Princess.

'Message from Savannah,' said Paige. 'We've got to go long. Legs are so out. Have you got anything maxi?'

'But my legs are my best feature!' said Lacey.

'I thought your back was your best feature,' I said.

She made a face. And then, 'Can I borrow your blue dress?'

'No.'

'It's for one night.'

'I'm using it,' I said.

'Fine. I'll just have to go shopping.'

'Oooh, can I come?' said Paige.

'Yes!' said Lacey. 'Are you free tonight? We could go to Cindy's, get some ideas.'

'I've got dance tonight. When's the concert?'

'The ninth,' said Lacey. 'So I suppose we could go tomorrow. Or . . .'

'The *ninth* of *July*,' I said. 'That date sounds sort of familiar, doesn't it, Lace?'

'Does it?'

'Yes. Are you sure it's not ringing any bells with you?'

She thought, for a second. 'Nope. God, Katie, why are you being so weird? If you want to come, come!'

And in my head I was screaming, *I don't want to come!*

What I want is for you to realize that it's my birthday that night and to say that of course you'd rather hang out with me and maybe at the same time you could admit that Karamel are bad and Savannah and co. are annoying and perhaps you could stop with all the leg and limo chat while you're at it!

Even Nirvana wouldn't be angry enough for this.

 53

CHAPTER SIX

Happy birthday to me

Happy birthday to me

Happy birthday, dear Katie

Happy birthday to me.

It's important I have that there because NO ONE ELSE SANG IT.

To be fair, Mum did at least have a present waiting on my plate when I finally staggered downstairs. (A pair of earrings with real diamonds in them! Teeny-weeny ones, but still!)

And Adrian had got me the reissue of *Frank* on vinyl, which was waiting in a flat, shiny square next to my place, underneath birthday cards from Gran and Auntie Tasha, who isn't a proper auntie, she's Mum's mate from nursing college, but hey, it's always good to have an extra auntie.

'Do you like it?' said Adrian, his early-morning face sporting a light coating of silver-and-black pre-beard.

I ripped off the paper. 'Yes! Yes I do!'

He did a whole playing-the-drums mime thing and ended with a *ba-doom-tish*. 'Get in.'

Now, me and Adrian had had our ups and downs recently, pretty steep ups and downs, come to think of it, what with him being Mum's new bloke and my self-appointed manager. And a nasty habit of coming downstairs in the mornings wearing Mum's flowery dressing gown.

Still, things had been getting better. And it was sweet that he cared so much about making me happy.

Yeah. Adrian was all right.

Manda had been in the bathroom when I woke up, and in the bathroom while I got dressed. She'd still been in there when I banged on the door and said that I had to clean my teeth, and do certain other things, quite urgently. She'd still been in there when I'd gone to do them in the downstairs loo, which I try to avoid at all costs, because there's a serious risk that people in the kitchen might overhear.

When she finally came in, she was holding something behind her back.

'Happy birthday, K-Star. Fourteen! Sorry I wouldn't let you into the bathroom. I was doing . . . this.'

 55

She handed me a package covered in about twenty different layers of tissue paper and trailing loads of swirly ribbons.

'Mands,' I said. 'Please don't tell me that you've spent the morning wrapping up a poo.'

She laughed. 'Come on. Open it!'

So I did . . . and . . .

'Well?' Her eyes were all glowy. 'What do you think?'

There in front of me was a brand-new leather-covered notebook, with my name on the front in letters that had been sort of pushed into the leather. And next to it, a pen in a little box.

'It's for your songs!' said my sister. 'I know you're always trying to write in that ratty old notebook, so I thought this might inspire you!'

No . . . no, no, no.

I mean, it was gorgeous. It had the new-leather smell that, in the normal way of things, I can't get enough of. And the covers were buttery soft. Then inside, page after pristine page of thick, creamy-white paper.

But if I couldn't write in just my normal lyric book, which was a battered, card-covered thing, how on earth was I meant to come up with something good enough to put on to these perfect pages?

It deserved someone so much better.

'This is . . . beautiful,' I managed, about ten seconds after I should've done.

'Good,' she said. 'I'm so glad I found something you can use.'

She knew from my face that I couldn't use it.

'It must have been expensive,' I said.

'It was.'

'Thank you so much.'

'All right,' said Amanda.

'So, Katie, what's the plan for your bash tonight?' said Adrian. 'I can go to Asda on the way back from the shop, just tell me what you need.'

'OK, right,' I said. 'A tub of Häagen-Dazs, any flavour you like so long as there's no fruit in it – I do not want my pleasure being ruined by anything even approaching a vitamin – plus Jaffa Cakes and a litre of Diet Coke . . . no wait, not diet, not today.'

'Enough sugar to send you to an early death – got it,' said Adrian. 'And how many pizzas? Is that Savannah girl going to be coming?'

'She's not coming,' I said. 'And –' this was surprisingly

hard to say – 'nor is Lacey.'

'Not coming to your birthday? Why not?'

'Because they're going to a Karamel concert,' I said, feeling really quite bleak. 'It's my fault; I got them tickets.'

Mum went to ask some probably very sensible question, so I held up my hands. 'Just . . . don't.'

'So, it'll be you and Amanda?'

'I dunno. I mean, I had this whole night planned, with *NOW* albums one to thirty-seven and dancing and stuff. But if Lacey's not going to be there, it's just you and me, Mands.' I sighed. 'You probably won't want to . . .'

Which was Amanda's cue to say that of course she wanted to, that we didn't need Lacey, that my big sis would be looking out for me, making absolutely sure that even though things had gone a little bit wrong my birthday would still be completely ace.

'Well, if you're not keen,' said Amanda, fiddling with a bit of abandoned tissue paper. 'Maybe we should leave it for this year.'

What? No!

'I mean, you're getting a bit old to dance around in your bedroom anyway, aren't you?'

No no no!

'I suppose so,' I said.

'OK then,' said Amanda.

It was interesting, because as I was unwrapping my earrings, I thought I'd never be unhappy again. Now, less than twenty minutes later, I was.

And that, ladies and gentlemen, was my special day.

Oh, no, wait – I missed the whole other middle part.

Probably because I've been trying to block it out.

I did consider pulling a sickie, but I knew Lace would have something special planned. And as I wasn't seeing her that evening, I thought I ought to let her make a fuss of me during the day.

My uplifting birthday breakfast meant I was running horribly late. So late that even though I got ready in double-quick time, I had to run if I wasn't going to miss the bus. Running is hard work, especially now that I'm getting on a bit.

'Happy birthday, by the way,' said Jaz, as we took our places: her on the back seat; me wheezing and sweating on the next row along – because, while I aspire to be a back-seat person, I don't think I'm there quite yet.

'Thanks,' I said, slightly surprised that she even knew about it.

'So –' Jaz folded herself up like the time Mum had caught a massive spider in a shot glass, her boots very much defying the sticker that said *Please Keep Your Feet off the Seats* – 'what does Katie do to celebrate her birthday?'

'I, um, have a dance party,' I said, worrying a little that Jaz would think I was a complete juvenile, but somehow it was too early in the morning to think of a decent lie. 'Me and Mands and Lacey all jump around to some vintage pop. Well, that's what I normally do. Only, this year . . .' I tailed off. 'That's what I normally do.'

Jaz considered the supreme patheticness of a Katie Cox dance party.

'That sounds bearable. What time?'

Jaz? At my dance party?

'Um, it's not really . . . a you kind of thing. It's more for me and Lacey and Manda. You know.'

'Yeah, I know,' repeated Jaz, staring out the window as though she was bored to death, which she probably was.

Then, because I hadn't been getting the bus for very long and it's important to find out this stuff, 'Do you lot have any special birthday rituals I should know about?'

'Like what?'

'Only, when I walked in along the canal, generally, if it was your birthday, you got chucked into the canal.'

'Oh. Right. No,' said Jaz. 'I mean, we couldn't do that on the bus anyway.'

'No,' I said. 'It would have to be something humiliating but non-messy. I guess we could draw all over someone with eye-pencil. You'd have to hold them down first, but . . .' I caught myself. 'OR, we could just be nice to whoever's birthday it is. Like normal people.'

'Nah,' said Jaz. 'Hey, you lot.' She was talking to the year sevens. 'Hold Katie down, yeah? And Nicole, get your eyeliner.'

'Happy birthday,' said Lacey, as I arrived in the form room, my face wet and covered with tiny flecks of loo roll, plus quite a lot of Nicole's eyeliner.

'Thanks, BFF,' I said, settling down at my desk. Then, in a whisper, 'Erm, Lacey? Just how bad do I look right now?'

'Pretty bad,' said Lacey. 'Your face is grey and splotchy and covered with bits of white stuff – what is that? And your fringe is all over the place. Why?'

I pretended to examine my fingernails. 'Because Dominic Preston is *looking at me*.'

Lacey peered over her bag. 'He is,' she said. 'You should smile or something. Look casual. But interested. And happy.'

'Like this?'

'What are you even doing with your mouth?'

'This is my casual-interested-happy smile,' I hissed.

'Never make that face again. Never, never, never.'

'Hey, Katie,' said Dominic. 'You OK?'

'YES!' I shouted.

'OK,' said Dominic, and then he went back to talking to Devi.

Me and Lace started to giggle.

'He is so into you,' said Lacey. 'Don't forget me once the two of you are going out.'

'I don't think that's very likely.'

'Well, maybe this'll help you remember,' said Lace. She reached into her bag and came out holding a little wrapped box.

'Oooh,' I said, jiggling it around, then picking it open. 'Oooh . . . a charm bracelet! Lace!'

'They've just got them in at Samuel's,' said Lacey,

looking extremely pleased with herself. 'I got four charms: a guitar, that's because of how you play the guitar . . .'

'An ice cream!'

'They didn't do Magnums, so that sort of represents them. And a microphone, and one of those squiggly things you get on music.'

'A treble clef?'

'If you say so.'

'Aw, Lace,' I said, thinking I might cry. And then quite wanting to, because it would show her how happy I was. Which meant, of course, that my eyes immediately dried up again. 'It's beautiful.'

'I tried to get something to be our Chinese takeaways, but they only had this Chinese-symbol one and I didn't know what it meant so I thought I'd better not.'

'Yeah,' I said. 'Like the one that Karamel lead singer has on his arm. I bet it means "I am a bum-face". Like, why have a tattoo in a language you don't understand?!'

'Um.' She looked away. 'I realized, last night . . . the concert, your birthday . . . talk about bad timing.'

Thank the Lord.

'Yeah,' I said.

'Why didn't you just tell me?'

 63

'Because I didn't want to spoil your amazing fun night with Savannah and co.'

'But if you'd said something at the time . . .' She was looking at me, her face all open and kind. 'Katie, I feel terrible.'

'It's OK!' I insisted. 'I've got it all planned out! We're going to have our regular dance party, unfortunately Mands is unavailable, but that just means extra pogoing space, and Mum and Adrian said we can make as much noise as we like.'

'Yay! It's going to be brilliant, Katie. We'll bust some moves and have proper Coke, and pizza, and ice cream – whatever you want. Plus, I've got this major new lip stuff we need to try; it puffs up your mouth like crazy. You can't even get it in shops, it's that good.'

I fastened the bracelet around my wrist. 'I knew you'd understand, Lace. You're the best friend ever.'

'Compliment accepted,' said Lacey. 'And the good thing about doing it tomorrow is that we have extra time to look forward to it.'

'Um . . . tomorrow? But I thought . . . you would . . . cancel . . . because . . .'

Her expression made me stop.

'Katie, I can't back out now. I promised Savannah. She's booked a limo!'

'Oh . . . OK.' It came out a bit wobbly.

She put her hand on my arm and looked me full in the face. 'Katie, it's just twenty-four hours.'

'It's fine,' I said. Translation: *It is not fine.*

Lacey speaks fluent Katie. Or, I thought she did.

'And I'm going to text you from the concert.'

'Cool.' Translation: *Please don't.*

'And I'll be thinking of you tonight. Thanks so much for the tickets.'

'No problem. Just going to pop to the loo before French.' Translation: *I am about to burst into tears.*

CHAPTER SEVEN

So that was it, really. Katie's Birthday Spectacular.

By the time I got up to my bedroom – after a special dinner, hand-cooked by Adrian, of slightly-past-its-sell-by-date ham-and-pineapple pizza and too much Häagen Dazs – I was pretty much over it.

So I crawled into bed and snapped off the light, ready to sleep it out.

It didn't work. Possibly because it was only seven thirty.

Fine. Maybe now was the moment to write that song for Tony.

I pulled my guitar out from underneath my hoodie and . . .

No.

Nothing.

I don't really understand about writing songs.

When it's going well, it's like the music is just there, inside of me, or maybe inside of my guitar, waiting for me to set it free. I don't notice that I'm trying to come up with rhymes or that the chords don't quite fit, because time's standing still and also going at triple speed.

It's not an easy thing to explain. All I can say is that although I know I'm working really hard, I don't even notice.

When it's going badly, though . . . it's like I'm made of the wrong stuff. Like my fingers are someone else's and the music's all drained out of my guitar, as though words are strange, spiky tools and I don't know how to use them.

No, that doesn't even begin to cover it. There's this sneaking feeling I get, that I've never really been able to write, that every other song I've managed was an accident, a fluke, or perhaps something I'd stolen without realizing.

It's like when you get insomnia. You know you've gone to sleep before. That every night of your life until now, you've just turned over and done it. Only, you can't remember how, and the more you think about it, the more impossible it feels, like someone's asking you to fly or go invisible.

It's like a part of me has died. Or maybe was never really there in the first place.

Superstar?

Super failure, more like.

My new phone went *ding!*

And there was a Lacey-Savannah-Paige-Sofie selfie: four pouty duck faces in front of a gigantic pink limousine, along with the words:

HEY KATIE, WE'RE HERE!

I threw my guitar across the room.

Then went and picked it up, because the evening was being bad enough without me breaking that as well.

What was wrong with them? Karamel weren't even slightly decent at the best of times. How could they be better than spending time with me on my fourteenth birthday?

Ding!

Now they were posing next to a gigantic gold letter 'K'.

EXCITED!!!!

Great, Lacey. I am glad that missing my birthday in order to hang out with the band I hate most in the world is making you so very happy.

> **LOOK! OOOOOOH!**

And now a photo of the poster filled my screen, three big stupid boy faces with even bigger, stupider boy hair.

Not only were they the worst and most annoying set of people in the actual universe, they were also quite literally ruining my life with their very existence.

Karamel, with their croony rubbish about how much they loved their mums and their bandmates and the invisible, imaginary girl standing in front of them.

Karamel, who always seemed to be photographed fooling about on the beach. Or in a swimming pool. Or on a bouncy castle.

Karamel, who seemed to start every song sitting on barstools.

Karamel, who—

Ding!

> **OMG K I CANNOT BELIEVE U R MISSING THIS!!!!!!**

Another selfie, this time of Lacey looking crazily flushed in front of the stage, with three lit-up blobs in the background. Honestly, the way she was going, she'd run out of exclamation marks.

Ding!

THIS IS THE BEST NITE OF MY LIFE!!!!!!!!!!!!!!!!

And the worst night of mine.

SAY SOMETHING KATIE

What could I say?

What *was* there to say?

And then . . .

And then . . .

I found that I had quite a lot of things to say, after all.

Can't stand the boy band
Plastic faces, stupid hair
Can't stand the boy band
The matching clothes they wear

The tattooed Chinese symbols
On the skin that's perma-tanned
I can't stand the boy band

Ding!

IM SO HAPPY RITE NOW THANK U THANK U THANK U

Don't like the boy band
Singing songs about their nans
Don't like the boy band
Hanging round their camper vans

Their lyrics are predictable
Their music's oh so bland
I don't like the boy band

Maybe this song was already inside me, waiting. Perhaps it had spent the last few months growing, feeding on the drip drip of loathing that I'd swallowed every time Savannah professed her undying love for them, or Paige sighed and said 'swoon'.

It certainly felt that way. My guitar seemed to offer up the chords before I even thought of them, and the chorus was right there, as though I was climbing a ladder and each word was a rung, easy, within reach, leading me up and on.

Oh poor sweet boy band
Your music makes me heave
You poor sad boy band
Soon one of you will leave

And if you think you'll be remembered
Then you misunderstand
RIP the boy band.

What had I been so worried about?

Songwriting was *easy*.

Ding!

KATIE WHATS THE MATTER?
TELL ME WHATS WRONG PLEASE

My fingers went to reply.

And then, I thought, no. I can do better than that.

If she wants to know, I'll tell her.

I propped my phone up on an empty tissue box, and started the voice recorder.

Then I picked up my guitar, and I began to sing.

Can't stand the boy band
Plastic faces, stupid hair . . .

And as I sang, I got angrier and angrier, until I could almost feel the threads of fire trailing from my fingertips as I slashed at the strings.

So angry, in fact, that by the time I'd finished, I was a tiny bit breathless and I could feel my cheeks pulsing, magma-hot underneath the back of my hand.

Done. Finished.

For a second, I hesitated. After what happened last time . . .

Only then, I thought, *No, it's fine. I'm not sticking it online or anything. I'm not actually mad. I'm just going to send it to a friend.*

I knew that it wasn't my best idea ever. That it would probably cause a row with Lace. But that was fine. In a slightly twisted way, it's what I wanted.

At least, it was at that precise moment. It probably wouldn't be once I'd had a chance to calm down.

Better send it now, then.

Very quickly, before I could change my mind, I opened a new message to Lacey, attached the file, and hit send.

And then . . . then I somehow felt a bit flat.

The song must have got all the mad stuff out of my system, like when you pop a spot and what was tight and inflamed before goes back to normal again, with just a gungy wodge of cotton wool and a bit of redness to show that anything was wrong in the first place.

Ding!

Here we go.

I reached for my phone, only then Mum's voice came shouting up the stairs.

'Katie? Something's . . . Katie! Get down here. Katie? Katie!'

I gulped. It takes a lot for Mum to be freaked out.

'Katie! Are you . . . Can you . . . Katie? Katie Katie Katie!'

Mum was totally freaking out.

'What is it?' I said, opening my bedroom door and edging across the landing to peer down the stairs. 'What's happened?'

'Hello, Katie.'

There, standing on the doorstep, surrounded by suitcases, was Dad.

CHAPTER EIGHT

'Oh my God!'

It's hard for me to describe Dad, because he's just basically Daddish to me. But if a stranger had been there too, they'd have seen:

A smiling man with loads of black hair, wearing a grey cotton shirt with the top three buttons undone. Decent jeans, and a belt with a big buckle that I'd not seen before, so possibly that was a thing he'd picked up in America. Only, he wasn't in America any more. He was right in front of me.

'Katie!'

Then I was pelting down the stairs and hurling myself into his arms, hugging him so tight that if it was anyone else I'd have been afraid of breaking them, but not Dad – Dad who was so tall and real and wonderfully, amazingly *here*.

'This is the best birthday surprise ever!'

'Is it . . . yes! Happy birthday!'

And we might have stood like that forever, or at least

a good couple of minutes, only we were interrupted by Mum saying:

'What the hell, Benjamin?'

He stood back, and I saw that he looked tanned, and thin . . . and tired.

Oh, Dad.

'Good to see you too, Zoe.'

'You can't just turn up out of the blue like this. I have a life now; you've no right to just waltz back in and –'

He took a step back, puzzled. 'But Katie said she'd . . .' They both looked at me. 'Katie, you said you'd tell her I was coming . . . ?'

'Ah. Um. Yes. Mum, Dad's coming back.'

'Katie . . . I . . .'

Mum isn't often lost for words. I somehow knew she'd make up for it later.

'Hello hello? Who's this, then?'

Adrian came through the hall, and stopped.

'This,' said Mum, 'is Benjamin. My ex-husband.'

'Well, he can't stay on the doorstep,' said Adrian, sticking out one of his big thick hands. 'Nice to meet you, Benjamin. I'm Ade. Come on in.'

▶

Then actual Dad was standing in my actual lounge, peering up at the cracks in the ceiling.

'How long have they been there?'

'Since we moved in,' I said, just as Mum said:

'Couple of days.'

He sucked his teeth. 'That's not good. You should get someone round.'

'Thanks for the input, Benjamin,' said Mum. 'Any other thoughts on our accommodation? While you're here?'

Dad's never been good at picking up sarcasm, and his stint stateside clearly hadn't improved matters, because he said, 'You should knock through, get a bit of light in. Open things up – you've got the dimensions but the furniture's too big, it feels cramped. And that's quite the drainage problem in the garden.'

Mum's knuckles were going white. Luckily, Adrian was between them.

'It's a proper doer-upper, that's what it is, Benj. Great to have your views on the place, actually; we're still at the ideas stage. Beer?'

'Got any wine open?' said Dad. 'A nice Shiraz would just hit the spot.'

Adrian chucked him a can of Tetley's. Dad caught it,

just, and we all waited. Then, he opened it, and sat down on the sofa.

I sat down too. And so did Adrian.

Mum stayed standing up.

'So, Katie tells me you're a musician,' said Adrian. 'Must be where she gets it from.'

'Yeah, yeah, mainly session work,' said Dad. 'But it keeps me busy. Just got out the studio last week, we were doing this huge stint on a new album, all very secret, of course, can't tell you much about it, but let's just say that a certain Miss Alicia Keys will be gracing the airwaves pretty soon with someone you know rather well.'

'Really?' I squeaked. 'Dad, that is so cool!'

'It's just work,' said Dad. 'I don't even get excited about it any more, to be honest.'

'You should do,' I told him.

He gave me a squeeze. 'Maybe.'

'Adrian is a very successful retailer,' said Mum. 'He owns Vox Vinyl!'

'It's just a little shop in town,' said Adrian.

'He's taking over the unit next door,' said Mum.

'And then, the world!' said Adrian.

'Great,' said Dad. 'So, Katie, would you like Alicia's autograph?'

'WOULD I?! Dad, that is so amazing! Best present ever!'

His hand went to his pocket and I thought my heart might stop then and there. 'Thought so. I'll let her know.' He tapped out a quick message, just as I heard the front door go. Manda.

'We're in the lounge,' I called.

I could hear her taking off her boots and then the double thump as she chucked them under the stairs. 'Any pizza left? Because – uuuuh.'

She was in the doorway, and she sort of began to crumple, her hands clutching against the wood as though the sight of Dad had been a punch.

'Dad? What are you . . . ?' She shook her head. 'Dad.'

He got to his feet, and, I dunno, maybe it was that she'd got older or that he'd got thinner, but I saw for the first time the way their hair curled up at the ends, that funny shrug they both do when they're embarrassed, the way their eyes have that little crease, just underneath, in the shadows.

He held out a hand. 'Come here, sweetheart.'

And, what do you know, she burst into tears.

Proper long sobs, as Mum and Adrian looked at their feet.

He put his arms around her and she shook and I knew exactly how she felt.

'Amanda, angel, it's OK.'

She dabbed at her eyes, and then, after I passed her a tissue, her nose.

'How come you're here?'

He looked at me. 'Katie, did you tell *anyone* I was coming? Anyone at all?'

I didn't quite know what to say, so I just made a face.

'Well, no harm done,' said Dad. 'I'm here now.'

'No harm done?' said Amanda, the tissue dropping to the floor. '*No harm done?*'

'Sorry,' I murmured.

'Dad, why didn't you tell me? You know what Katie's like.'

'I didn't . . . we'd not spoken in a while. So . . .'

'We'd not spoken because I can never get you on the phone!' She wiped her nose on the back of her wrist and glared.

'Work's been crazy, and there's the time difference. And I know you have a job now. I can't just ring you whenever.'

'You can, Dad,' said Amanda.

'OK, then,' said Dad. 'From now on, I will.'

'Great.'

There was a long pause. I got to work filling it. 'Er, Mands, what do you mean, "You know what Katie's like"?'

'Oh, you know.' She flapped an irritated hand. 'Useless.'

'What? How can you say that? I'm not the one who bailed on her little sister ON HER FOURTEENTH BIRTHDAY.'

'That is not what we are talking about.'

'Then what *are* we talking about?'

This was turning into one of those arguments that you never remember starting and so can't ever finish.

'Just . . . shut up, Katie.'

Dad took a step forward. 'Don't talk to your sister like that.'

'Brilliant,' said Amanda. 'You run off to America and now you're back and you're trying to *discipline* me? I'm going to bed.'

When she slammed the door, it bounced a few times, and then fell off its hinges.

'So,' said Dad, who was going for the Let's Pretend None of That Just Happened way of dealing with things.

 81

'Is someone going to give me a tour?'

'It's late,' said Mum. 'Maybe you should head off to . . . wherever you're staying . . . and we'll do the tour another time.'

This is when it occurred to me that there was another part of Dad's message I'd failed to deliver.

'Well, actually, Mum, I sort of said he could stay here. With us.'

Dad did the shruggy, grinny thing that he does.

Mum started to inflate.

I went into crash position in my head.

Only then, before she could blow, Adrian nodded.

'Sure you can, mate. Plenty of room in the den, so long as you don't mind a few mushrooms. Want to follow me? I'll get you all set up.'

Off they went.

'Katie—' Mum began.

'Oh dear, is that the time? I'm so very tired,' I said.

And before they could stop me, I was scarpering back up the stairs to my room and shutting the door and ignoring Amanda who was staring out the window at the rain, and pulling my cover over my head and sticking my headphones in my ears and noticing as I did that I had twenty-five missed calls from Lacey.

Was I in the mood to hear how fabulous her evening had been?

No.

No, I was not.

I lay there, in the dark, hearing my breath flutter, in, out, in, out.

Dad was back.

Here.

Home.

Maybe it hadn't been such a bad birthday after all.

My Dad

My dad rocks hard
My dad is ace
My dad plays lead guitar
And drums and sax and bass

My dad's way cool
My dad's so fine
My dad lives his dreams
And shows me mine

Wish I'd seen his stateside pad
Yeah, I bet that flat was rad
I'm glad
So glad
He's my dad

My dad was gone
My dad went away
My dad, across the ocean
And the sky turned grey

I think of what we had

And all I feel is sad

But I'm glad

So glad

He's my dad

My dad was lost

My dad's been found

My dad spins the world

With his unique dad sound

My sister says he's bad

And he makes my mother mad

But still, I'm glad

So glad

He's my dad

I'm glad

So glad

He's my dad.

CHAPTER NINE

'Wake up, K.'

I opened my eyes to see a bit of morning sun, which was being blocked out by Amanda's great big face, so close that I could see the pores all round the edges of her nose. Pores that could really do with a clean, if we're being honest, which I was about to be, when—

'Can we talk? Or are you going to dive back under your duvet again?'

I *had* been about to dive back under the duvet, but in the interests of sisterly cooperation, I didn't.

'What do you want to talk about?'

'Dad. He's here. In this house. Downstairs. Right now.'

I remembered, and grinned, giving Mands an eyeful of my morningy teeth. 'Isn't it the best?'

'No,' said Amanda. 'It isn't. It's the opposite of that. Mum's in bits. And she said that you'd told him it would be OK to stay? What were you thinking?'

'I was thinking that it would be nice for us all to be together again,' I said.

 86

'So you weren't thinking,' said Amanda.

She was trying to look into my eyes, and I thought how strange it was that she couldn't see that this was Dad we were talking about. Our dad. Mine and hers. How strange, and how sad.

If she didn't understand this, then really, there was nothing else to say.

So I broke her gaze, and turned away to get dressed. By the time I'd finished, she was gone.

Probably for the best, I thought, as I went downstairs.

And there he was!

'Morning, my darling,' said Dad, sitting at the breakfast table and buttering himself a cinnamon bagel.

'Morning!' I sang, giving myself a celebratory double helping of Coco Pops.

'Morning all,' said Adrian. 'Um, Zoe said to apologize, but she's on an early shift today, so she'll see you all later.'

'I thought her early shift was next week,' I said.

'No,' said Adrian. 'It's today.'

'It's definitely next week,' I insisted, because it was.

'Avoiding me, is she?' said Dad.

Adrian gave me a look and I decided I'd shut up for a bit.

'Nasty leak you've had there,' said Dad, nodding at the weird marks on the ceiling above the fridge. 'You want to get that sorted out.'

'Yup, it's on the list,' said Adrian, and I suppose it was because it was so early that he sounded a tiny bit exhausted.

Dad went back to his bagel for a bit. Then, 'Hey, Katie, want a lift to school?'

'Total yes!' I thought about it for a second. 'Have you got a car? Already?'

'Nah, I'll take Adrian's. You don't mind, do you, Ade? Give us a chance to do a bit of father–daughter bonding.'

'But you're not insured, *Benj*.'

Dad gave him a playful smack in the stomach. 'Just this once.'

'But—'

'Oh, go on,' I said. Because, really, a chauffeured ride to school with Dad versus a bus trip watching Nicole waxing her arm hair with duct tape – it wasn't much of a contest.

Adrian made a grab for the worktop, but Dad's hand was already there. Then he was holding up the car keys.

'Ready when you are, Katie.'

So we whizzed past the bus stop and zoomed along

through the fields, and Dad drives far too fast, and it's brilliant. And then, way too soon, I was getting out on the double-yellow lines by school and heading for the form room, with a full six hours before I'd see him again.

'Katie,' said Lacey, staggering in and plunking herself down into her chair. 'Why are you not answering your phone?'

I wrenched my mind back from The Amazing Dad Show and tried to focus. 'I've been . . . quite . . . busy.'

'You're stropping about your birthday, aren't you? I knew you would and you are.'

'Am I?'

'Honestly, Katie, get over it.'

'I'm over it,' I said. Then, as I really digested what she'd said, 'It's been kicking off a bit at home, that's all.'

'Ri-iiight,' Lacey folded her fingers under her chin and sighed, and I gradually became aware she was waiting for me to ask her something. I wasn't sure what, so I just said:

'So . . . what's the . . . you know . . . ?'

Lacey sighed. 'The concert was just . . .' She searched for the right word. 'Like . . . I mean, when they sing, Katie. I thought I'd die. Honestly, I did. We were in the middle of the front row and when Kurt did "Beautiful Girl" he looked straight at me and—'

'Ah,' I said, as it all came back to me, like a boomerang comes back and smacks you round the face. 'Karamel.'

'Yes, Karamel.'

Now I was remembering, I preferred it when I'd forgotten.

'I cried,' said the idiot who had apparently taken possession of my best friend. 'I actually cried.'

'Right.'

'When you see them, live, it's . . . it's . . .' She shivered. 'I'm shivering just thinking about it.'

'Maybe you should go to the sick room.'

'So, afterwards, we went backstage – we had these wristbands that they gave us, I'm never cutting mine off!'

She waved it at me.

It was just a wristband.

'Do go on,' I said.

Lacey went on. And on, and on. Stuff about dance moves and photographers and after-parties and blah blah blah-de-blah.

'And then as we were going back to the limo, I listened

she'd got home, but just clambered into some kind of Barbie packaging and slept standing up.

'Katie, have you HEARD?'

'Heard what?'

'Amaze,' said Savannah.

'What?' I said. 'Spit it out. We have to get to English.'

'Shall I tell her?' said Lacey, as though I wasn't even there.

'No, I'll do it,' said Savannah. 'Katie. Are you ready? Because this changes everything.'

I was finding it very hard to be the chilled-out person I usually am. 'What changes what?'

'I'm going out with Kolin. From Karamel. KolinfromKaramel.'

'Oh, right,' I said.

This was clearly not the reaction Savannah had been expecting.

'I am going out with Kolin from Karamel.'

'Yes, I'm with you.'

'She doesn't care,' said Lacey. 'You know how she feels about them. It's like she's missing part of her brain, or something.'

'Or you are,' I murmured.

Savannah didn't show any sign of having heard me. 'So, after the show, we all go to the party, and I can feel someone looking at me. And it's him! It's Kolin! And we talked and talked and it turns out we like loads of the same things and then he gave me his number and I gave him mine and now he's my boyfriend.'

'That's great, Savannah,' I said. 'You two sound perfect for one another. You like Karamel, he's in Karamel. It's a match made in heaven.'

Once, Lacey would have laughed.

Now, she said:

'Maybe it is.'

Then, the two of them fell into step ahead of me, Savannah's gold-plated phone glinting between them, like a stupid expensive phone that had been covered in stupid expensive gold.

'Our pics have been getting some major play,' Savannah said. 'Like, *major* major.'

'Wow,' said Lacey.

I dropped back a bit. They'd probably slow down and wait for me.

'Oooooh, Kol posted the fairy-lights one! I am so glad he is my boyfriend.'

'Yay, me too!'

It was almost as though they preferred to talk to each other than to me!

'Oof, the Karamel fans are sooooo jealous,' said Savannah. 'Total eeek. I'd probably better change my profile name.'

'And maybe not have your avi be the one of you kissing Kolin,' said Lacey.

'Let's not go crazy,' said Savannah. 'I mean, I'm, like, not going to let the haters control my life, you know? Just because I am lucky enough to have someone from a very major band as my boyfriend. I cannot live a lie.'

'No,' said Lacey.

Then:

'Oh no. No, no, no.'

'No! Nooooooo!'

They stopped and turned, and a very pathetic part of me actually felt grateful for a bit of eye contact.

'Katie,' said Lace. 'You need to see this.'

Savannah held up her phone.

It was the feed from *Kurt_Karamel*.

'No,' I said. 'I do not want to hear about last night any more.'

'K! This is important!'

'It's not! It's really not.'

'Um, actually, Katie . . .'

'How are we still talking about this?' I said, in this semi-shriek. 'Yay, you went to see Karamel. Woo, you partied backstage. Squee, Kolin and Savannah are now an item. I'm. Not. Interested.'

'Is she OK?' said Savannah. 'She doesn't seem OK. Katie, are you OK?'

'I'm *fine*,' I said. 'But I would be even more fine if we could just talk about something else.'

People were stopping and turning round.

'Look at it, Katie.' Lacey's voice was serious.

'No!'

'You have to look!'

'NO!'

'KATIE YOU HAVE GOT TO READ THIS.'

'So what?'

'*Read it.*'

The screen was right in front of my eyes, and I focused in long enough to see:

Kurt_Karamel

Hey there.

Found out about this last night.

Kinda upset as I was a big fan of hers.

Peace and love

Kurt x ·

And underneath was a link.

The phone began to sing, in my voice:

Can't stand the boy band . . .

Kurt had posted my song.

CHAPTER TEN

'Ha ha ha ha ha,' said Jaz. 'You insulted Karamel. Ha ha ha ha ha ha ha ha ha. Ha ha ha ha ha ha ha ha ha.'

There was quite a lot more of this, but it's way boring written down.

We were on the bus, because despite promising me a lift home – 'While I'm around, my princess will not be getting public transport' – Dad failed to materialize. I'm guessing Adrian wanted his car back, which is kind of selfish.

Anyway, me and Jaz were down the back, watching Nicole trying to hack some false nails from her fingers.

'She didn't realize it costs twenty-five quid to get them taken off again,' said Jaz, as Nicole attacked them with the end of a compass.

The bus went over a bump and I looked away. The windows were smeary on the inside and the outsides were coated with these vague grey spots of yuk.

Then, a cheer. 'First one's off!' said Fin.

'Great!' I said, hoping that there hadn't been too much collateral damage.

 98

Then Jaz remembered about the Karamel thing again. 'But how did he get hold of the song? I thought you only sent it to Lacey.'

'I did,' I said, a tiny area of my brain registering that Jaz sounded a bit hurt, but really, there was no time for that now. 'I sent it in a private message.'

'Then how did he . . . ?'

I thought back to that terrible moment a couple of hours earlier, as we all stood outside the English room, staring at each other.

'Lace, did you send it to Kurt?'

'Of course I didn't!' said Lacey. 'How could I?'

Long pause.

'I did send it to Sofie, though. It was too noisy to hear it properly in the limo so she wanted to listen when she got home.'

We all turned to Sofie.

'I only sent it to Devi Lester,' she said.

'How did Devi Lester . . . ? Why Devi Lester? And how did it get from Devi to—'

'OK, that would be me.' Paige let out this fluttery laugh. 'So, Devi has this really fun messenger group, it's so fun, Katie, you should get him to add you, anyway, he has this

group and whenever he finds something fun, he shares it and normally it's just Nicole squeezing spots or whatever, but this time, it was you, which is fun, so Devi sent it out and I saw it and I was all, like, "ooooh" and I kind of sent it to Mum because she's a fan of yours.'

'Yeah,' said Jaz, who was clearly starting to get a bit bored of this story. 'So that's how it got from Devi to Paige's mum. But how did it go from Paige's mum to Kurt from Karamel?'

'I'm getting to that,' I said. 'So, Paige's mum, apparently, sent it to Cindy, you know Cindy? She runs that shop, in town. Cindy's. And Cindy sent it to . . .'

'Savannah.'

Savannah looked up from her phone and smiled. 'What?'

'Savannah, did you send Kurt from Karamel an MP3 of Katie being mental?'

'No!' said Savannah.

'Then, how . . . ?'

'I sent it to Kolin!' She applied a tiny bit of Lancôme juicy tube and smacked her lips. 'He's my boyfriend.'

I was brought back to the bus by a volley of Jaz cackles.

'It's not that funny.'

'Isn't it?' said Jaz.

'Lacey's ready to kill me. And what about all their fans? I'm probably going to have to sleep with a baseball bat by my bed. And—'

'Katie, calm down. These are people who like Karamel.' Jaz tried not to smile, and failed. 'I suppose they might *snuggle* you to death . . .'

'Seriously, though. I was thinking, if I call Tony he can get them to take it down again, maybe we can get the police on it or something, I mean, it's stealing, isn't it? Sticking someone's song online without their permission. Isn't it?'

For a second she actually looked reasonably serious. 'Seriously? I've listened to it.'

'What! When?!'

'Just now. While you were talking.' She lifted up her hair to show an earbud, nestling deep in her ear.

'Oh.'

'And I think it's cool.'

Not that I was especially out to impress Jaz. But . . . 'Do you?'

'Yeah,' said Jaz. 'I do.'

I stared at Jaz's face, and thought how different she and Lacey were. With Lace, I know completely what she looks

 101

like, how she has a pointy chin and milky skin and freakily tiny ears. Jaz's face, even though I saw it every day, was still a bit of a mystery, with its massively pencilled brows and lumps of covered-up spots and angles of cheekbone that seemed to change according to her mood, or my mood, or the weather, or maybe according to how much blusher she was wearing.

And she thought my song was cool.

We'd reached my stop. So I got off.

With a house as vibrant and ever-changing as ours, there's always something new to enjoy. Last week there'd been the windowsill underneath Mum and Adrian's bedroom falling off and landing on top of the porch. At the weekend, Adrian had hacked back some of the ivy around the side, revealing that a bit of the house we'd thought had been made of bricks was actually just bits of board held together by a few rusty nails and half a 'For Sale' sign from 1996.

And today, there was a huge black car parked outside.

Huh.

I took a couple of deep breaths and then went in.

To see Tony Topper, head of Top Music, sitting next to

Dad, in our lounge, being handed a cup of tea by Adrian.

'Hi,' I said. 'Would you like some tea? Hang on, you've got tea. Would you like a biscuit?' *Stop talking, Katie.* 'We've only got Bourbons and they're a bit smashed up because I dropped the shopping.'

Tony very sensibly ignored all this, and just said, 'Katie, I hope you're well.'

He was so sharp and tanned that he made everything else seem sort of insubstantial, somehow. Like he was an actor and our house was a film set and if you gave the walls a push they'd tip over.

Which, come to think of it, they probably would.

'I come bearing good news,' he said, smiling with his white, white teeth. 'You're aware of the Teen Time Awards?'

'With the poppy bands and the cheesy presenters and the pathetic embarrassing concert at Wembley that's supposed to be spontaneous but everyone knows is rigged and rehearsed and the speeches that are always really heartfelt and sappy and basically make me want to puke?'

'Yes,' said Tony. 'That. You've won a Teen Time Award.'

'God, I hate them so much . . . Did you say I've won?'

'Yes. The People's Act. The people voted and they picked you.'

'Whaaaaaaaaaaaat?' If I'd been in a film it would have done that thing where the background rushes past and my face goes super close-up. 'I've *won* an *award*?'

'You've won the People's Act Teen Time Award, yes.'

'*I've won?*'

'Yes.'

'*I can't believe I've won!*'

'Well, you did.'

'*That's unbelievable!*'

'Believe it.'

'*I can't!*'

Tony turned to Adrian. 'Is she all right?'

'In my experience,' said Adrian, 'this might go on for a while. You can sometimes jolt her out of it by offering her a slice of pizza.'

I calmed down. 'It's just, I don't win things. I'm not a winning kind of a person. Like –' I tried to explain – 'if there's a tombola, say, I just know that I won't pick the right number. I physically can't. The winning tickets see my fingers coming and they recoil.'

'Maybe,' said Tony, taking a delicate sip of tea. 'But

this involved people casting votes. So it's not chance.'

'Huh,' I said. 'Huh.'

'The results stay secret until the night, of course, so keep it under your hat. In the meantime, stick the date in your diary and think which song you'd like to play. And – Katie? Are you . . . crying?'

'Sorry, it's just . . .' I was thinking of all those people, in their bedrooms, watching me and then bothering to vote. It was kind of amazing. 'I didn't know how it would feel. To have people love me. It's nice. That's all.'

Adrian gave me a pat on the back, and then Dad got up to give me a hug.

'I'm glad you're so pleased,' said Tony. 'And I have to say, this all bodes very well for your concert next week. As instructed, we've booked you a nice, intimate venue, a little place in Camden, seats a couple of hundred, tickets go on sale tomorrow and there's been plenty of interest. That, and your impending award, mean you've really got the wind behind you right now.'

'Great!' I decided I wouldn't think about the couple of hundred people. Or the performing part. Or, you know, anything.

'There's just one issue.' Tony looked for somewhere

to put his mug, considered the cardboard box we were using as a coffee table, and then gave up. 'We at Top Music were very interested to hear that you'd written and released a song.'

'Ah. The song. Yes.'

'Katie, you told me, back in the office, that you didn't have any new material.'

'Yeah, but—'

'And we'd worked very hard to come up with a list of things for you to write about.'

'Yes, but it was—'

'Then, instead, you write –' he wrinkled his nose – 'something else.'

'I didn't mean for it to get seen by everyone,' I said.

'So –' Tony leaned in as though he was talking to a particularly stupid child – *'why did you put it on the internet?'*

'I didn't! I literally sent it to one friend! My bes—' I stopped myself. 'One friend.'

'Karamel are the UK's most successful group. They're with Top Music, like you. They are your stablemates. And now I have to sit at my desk and justify to the world why our newest signing has publicly slated our biggest act.'

'I'm sorry,' I said. 'I didn't mean to make life difficult for other people. I just wanted to write a good song.'

'From now on, I'll decide if it's a good song,' said Tony. 'We can talk to Kurt, get that rant taken down. And replace it with . . . In fact, we've been working on a little something, if you'd like to take a look . . .'

He handed me a piece of paper, heavy and white, with 'Top Music' printed at the top, and my eyes scanned down to:

Getting late
Party's starting
See my mates
Music's playing

'Well?'

'It's all right,' I said, looking into my lap. Then, I don't know why, but it was like Jaz was sitting on my shoulder. Not a full-sized Jaz, obviously, that wouldn't work at all. A mini Jaz, whispering into my ear. Saying, 'I thought it was cool.'

'I'm sorry,' I said, and then, as tiny invisible imaginary Jaz rolled her eyes, 'I mean, not sorry. I am not sorry. I really like the song I've already written.'

Tony had been about to take another sip of tea, but he paused. So I carried on.

'It's just, musically, I'm actually pretty pleased with how it came out; it's got all this energy. And there's nothing else like it out there, is there?'

'Why do you think that is?' said Tony.

A vision of Lacey and Savannah, swinging up the corridor ahead of me, comparing selfies.

'I'll tell you why – it's because people are afraid to have an opinion. Everyone plays it safe all the time, so no one ever gets upset and everything sells to the maximum number of people. And you know what, OK, maybe this has annoyed some dorky Karamel fans. But so what? I believe in my lyrics.'

'I see,' said Tony.

'Great!' I said.

'Mmm,' said Adrian.

'Isn't Katie something?' said Dad. 'I wish I could say she'd got it from me.' He grinned around the room. 'I mean, I'm a musician myself, so in a sense, she did.'

'Is that right?' said Tony, distantly.

'Session work, for the last few years, you know how it is.'

'Uh huh.'

'In fact, if you ever need anyone, for anything . . .'

'Sure,' said Tony.

Dad was reaching round the back of the sofa for a guitar. 'Happy to give you a quick demo now, if you'd like. Or I can ping you a link, whatever's easier.'

'Um, Benjamin, mate, I think he's here for Katie,' said Adrian.

'It's fine,' I said. 'Dad's an amazing musician. You should totally listen to his stuff.'

Tony held up his hands. 'All right! I will!'

Dad relaxed back into his chair.

'So,' said Tony. 'Just for the record, Katie, I am asking you, one final time, to write a different song. Something positive. Will you do that?'

'But . . .'

'You said, just now, how nice it was to feel loved. Do you really want to put out a song that's all about hate?'

And for a second, I did think, maybe this man has a point. I mean, he was the head of a massive record label with all this experience, and there were a lot of Karamel fans. Perhaps, I could maybe have a go at writing something else. If not about partying all night then maybe about . . . cats . . . ?

That would make Lacey happy too. A song about cats, or dancing, or my awesome friends; it would have me back in everyone's good books. I could be BFFs with Lacey and mates with Savannah and Sofie and Paige and maybe we'd all ride around in a pink limo and I could wear tight clothes and love Karamel like everybody else. Top Music would write my songs and Savannah would pick my clothes and I'd go on a diet and . . .

'No,' I said. 'My next single is "Can't Stand the Boy Band". Exactly as I recorded it in my room.'

He got to his feet. 'All right then. I will do my very best to sell it.'

'Thank you,' I said, sort of in shock. Had I really *won*?

'Good luck, Katie.'

'Thanks! See you soon, Tony.'

And then he was out the door and the big black car was sliding away, leaving me and Adrian staring at each other.

'I hope you know what you're doing,' said Adrian.

'Can you give me Tony's email address?' said Dad.

CHAPTER ELEVEN

Tea that night should have been brilliant, what with having everyone round the table together.

Should have been, but wasn't.

Mum was shooting evils at me and Dad.

Amanda was ignoring Dad and shooting evils at me.

Adrian was giving me worried looks.

I was sending love vibes to Dad and trying to avoid Mum, Adrian and Manda altogether. It was doing terrible things to my digestion.

'Can I go up to my room?' I asked. 'I need to get ready for Lacey.'

Mum looked up. 'Lacey?'

'It's my birthday dance party,' I said. 'My belated birthday dance party.'

'Right,' said Amanda, in a way that made it clear she wasn't planning on joining us. 'Have fun.'

'Will do!' I said.

And then, because while I probably could have managed one more fajita, it might not have mixed well with the shapes I was planning to throw, I excused myself and went upstairs to prepare the dance floor.

One look down and I decided to give up. We could dance on top of the mess.

Instead, I lay on my bed, and waited for the doorbell.

And waited.

But it was nice to have a bit of me time. Get some headspace. Think about the last twenty-four hours.

Think about my new song. Think about what I'd done.

What *had* I done?

I decided that I wouldn't think about it.

My thumb went to my phone and hovered over Lacey's face.

> What time R U coming? ☺ K x

> Soz forgot. Am at Paige's. Come over!
> We r doing eyebrows and U r totally invited xx

Oh.

So much for my birthday dance party.

So much for best friendship.

Not only had she now doubly abandoned my birthday

celebrations, she was leaving me alone in my hour of need! My song was out there, doing its thing, and I was desperate for a bit of wisdom. Not a trip to Paige's house and an attack on my facial hair.

Which is when it hit me that Lacey was the worst possible person to help me face all this stuff. She would tell me to get rid of 'Can't Stand the Boy Band'. She'd probably even bring me a Karamel poster to stick over my bed.

There was another option, though. If I was feeling brave.

And, yeah. Why not?

Maybe don't think about that, either.

The reply came through almost before I'd hit send.

On my way
Jazzzzz x

Twenty minutes later, and Jaz was propped up against my bed with my laptop open. She'd made herself very much at home, stuffing my pillow into the small of her back and resting her muddy platform boots right in the centre of Amanda's face towel.

I remembered the last time she'd been in my room, with most of my family, and the impromptu jamming session that had lead to the release of 'Just Me', and locked the door.

'Have you gone to see the fallout yet?'

'I'm too . . .' I wanted to say that I was scared. But Jaz didn't need to hear that. So I just said, 'No. Not yet. Been quite busy.'

'OK then. Here we go.'

She typed my name, and whistled.

I pulled my jumper over my head, even though I could hear Mum's voice telling me that I was going to ruin it. Then, from inside my woolly tent, 'Is it bad? It's bad, isn't it? I've really upset people. Oh please don't let me get trolled, I can't bear it. Let's ring Tony and get him to take it down.'

'Katie, look.'

'I just . . . I don't know what I was thinking. Yes, I do. I was upset at Lacey and this was my way of getting back at her. But it's immature, it's . . .'

'Wow.'

'I'm sorry.'

'Don't be,' said Jaz. 'Really, look.'

I stuck my nose out, and then one eye. And . . .

LOVE IT.

Finally someone is telling the TRUTH

Stand up for real music!!!!!!!!!!!!!

she haz such a nice voice I luv her

will u follow me Katy I am yr biggest fan

**go 2 my site for KATIE COX CLIPS music wallpaper
and MORE**

Bet Kristian is first one to leave lol

'They like it,' said Jaz. 'The people of the internet are on your side. Well, not the Karamel fans – you're going to have to steer clear of them. Stay in your bubble.'

'My bubble?'

'You know,' said Jaz. 'Your corner. The Katie zone. Friends and fans and stuff.'

  115

'They honestly like it?'

'They think you rock.'

I looked. And, mad though it seemed, clearly, they did.

'That's unbelievable,' I said. 'I am in actual shock.'

'I don't get you, Katie,' said Jaz. 'I don't get you at all.'

Now this, coming as it did from the world's least gettable person, was a little on the surprising side.

'What don't you get?' I said, letting my other eye come out from under my jumper. And then the rest of me, because being half in and half out of a jumper is both difficult and uncomfortable.

'You write a song because you have something to say. And then, when people start agreeing, you're all, "really?" For the sake of your dignity, Katie, at least try to own it.'

Which stung.

'What should I do?' I said. 'If I'm going to, um, own it?'

'What do you want to do?' asked Jaz.

'Er, nothing?'

Wrong answer.

'How's this?' said Jaz, her black nails tapping at the keyboard.

'What? What did you put?' I leaned around her.

KTCoX: Hey Kurt_Karamel thnkx for posting my song. So nice of u ;) xox

'What? Don't say that! Jaz, what is wrong with you? You're out of control.'

She gave me one of her looks, and as she did, I considered how a message like this would look, to the world.

It would look as though I was kind of crazy.

And cheeky.

And confident.

And cool.

This, I realized, was why I'd invited Jaz over. She went to delete the words, and I held her arm. 'Actually, yeah, say that.'

She pressed return, and there it was.

I'd said it.

My insides did a little whoosh.

'I mean, it's not like he'll see,' I said, as much to myself as to her. 'He must have a squillion messages a minute, he's hardly going to—'

'He's replied,' said Jaz. 'Freak to the beat – Kurt from Karamel has REPLIED.'

Kurt_Karamel: Thought you were better than this.

We looked at each other, and I became aware that we were both squealing. I mean, not in a girly way, that's not really me, and it's certainly not Jaz. But if you had to pick a word to describe the noise we were making, the word would be 'squeal'.

Even as we were still making faces, my hands were on my laptop and this time I didn't stop until I'd hit return.

KTCoX: I like real music. Not yr soppy plastic gunk.

My eyes were dancing, while my head filled with this buzzing sound, and . . . no, it was my phone. My phone was buzzing.

'Lacey?' I felt a little kick of unhappiness. 'Aren't you *busy* tonight?'

'What are you doing?'

'Just hanging out with Jaz. Doing a bit of messaging. You know.'

'Leave Kurt ALONE.'

An hour ago she was too wrapped up with Paige and co. to talk to me. Now, though, now she was interested.

'Gosh, Lacey,' I said. 'Poor Kurt. I bet he's crying into his Karamel pillowcase.'

'He's a sensitive, kind, real person, Katie.'

'No, he's not. He's a famous person. They are not sensitive or kind. Everyone knows that famous people are selfish and annoying.'

'You're pretty famous,' said Lacey.

'What's that supposed to mean?'

A thump, followed by a flurry of giggles. 'Paige! I am trying to talk to Katie. This is important! Stop it. Stop it!'

Were they having a pillow fight? Life in the Savannah set seemed to be one long tampon advert.

'Come on, Lace,' I said. 'He's not a person like, say –' I tried to think of a person – 'um . . . Dominic Preston. And I couldn't care less about his pathetic fans.'

'Katie, you are . . .' Lacey searched around for the word, and I heard another thump, and then she hung up.

While I'd been wasting time with the new Savannah Mini Me, he'd come back for more.

Kurt_Karamel: My music means a lot to me. I write from the ♥

 119

My fingers raced across the keys, trying to keep up with my brain.

KTCoX: U write to make money7. From girls who don't know better

'Shame about the 7,' said Jaz.

Kurt_Karamel: Coming from the new Justin Bieber

'WHAT? I am not! Bieber is . . . I am NOT A BIEBER.'

'You did get famous by recording a video in your bedroom which then went viral and . . .' began Jaz, before seeing my face. 'No. Of course you're not.'

KTCoX: At least Im not a manufactured band who plays music writne in confrence rooms by middle aged men unlike SOMONE.

Kurt_Karamel: I don't need to defend my music to you.

KTCoX: Like you can call it music. U are the enemy of good music.

I hit return, then realized I hadn't finished.

People like u are—

Only, Jaz's hand was on top of mine. 'Shall we stop a minute?'

'What? Why? I was just getting going.'

'Yeah. I think you need to calm down,' said Jaz.

'I am perfectly calm, thank you very much.' I mean, I was breathing a bit heavily, and one of my legs had started twitching of its own accord, but, let's be clear, I was in full control of the situation. 'He's an idiot!'

'Yes. But –' Jaz considered my duvet cover – 'it's a bad idea to do this sort of thing when you're worked up. Hey, let's go through your sister's stuff instead.' Then, next thing I knew, she'd closed the laptop and was opening up Amanda's top drawer and laying out its contents on the bed.

'Um, I don't know if that's a good idea,' I said, trying to drag my head out of the sharp, shiny world inside

 121

my screen and into real life again. 'Mands is a total neat freak; she'll kill me if she thinks I've messed up her stuff.'

'And that affects me how?' said Jaz. 'Where's the juice?'

'Amanda doesn't have any juice,' I told her, as Jaz chucked a load of socks down on to the floor, where they were immediately sucked into the swamp. 'She's even less exciting than I am. You should probably put those back.'

'OK, I'm over this now,' said Jaz, who didn't seem in any hurry to put anything away. 'Shall I see if Nicole's about? She's been saying she wants to get her bellybutton pierced.'

'It's too late,' I said. 'Nowhere will be open.'

'Pierced by me,' said Jaz. 'You can watch, if you want. Take photos.'

'No thank you, Jaz,' I said, prising open my laptop. My life was complicated enough without Nicole's bellybutton bleeding all over it. 'I want to get back to Kurt.'

'Nah,' said Jaz, nudging it shut. 'You've done enough. Leave it now.'

'Seriously, I don't mind upsetting him. He deserves it. For crimes against the top one hundred.'

And now my heart was thumping, bang, bang, bang . . .

no, it was my bedroom door. My door was thumping.

'KATIE. KATIE. KATIE.'

'What?'

'I've got to get up early for work tomorrow,' said my sister's voice. 'So I would quite like some sleep.'

And even I could see that denying Manda access to her bed would lead to the kind of conversation I could do without.

'Maybe we *should* stop for the night,' I told Jaz. 'Thanks, though.'

'For what? I didn't do anything. That was all you.'

'Well, thanks anyway.'

I unlocked the door, and there was Amanda. I smiled at her, but her face, it was not smiling back. It was doing the very opposite of smiling, in fact.

'What the—'

We looked at the contents of her drawers, spread all over everything.

'You do not touch my stuff,' said Amanda, slowly, sounding sad and angry at the same time.

'I didn't mean—'

'See ya, then,' said Jaz, flitting past her, down the stairs and out the front door.

 123

'I thought we were doing OK, sharing,' said Mands. 'I trusted you. And now I find you going through my personal things, with *Jaz*, of all people . . .'

'Mands, it wasn't me; it was all her. She just started rummaging – there was nothing I could do.'

Amanda was shovelling her stuff out of my reach. 'Fine.'

And I wanted to tell her what had just happened. I wanted, no, needed, to talk to her, to work out whether any of this was OK. In fact—

'Katie, shut your laptop and go to sleep.'

And in case I was still in any doubt about her feelings, she turned out the light.

My World

Life is better
In my phone
While it's on
I'm not alone

In my laptop
Feels more real
My fingers talk
Say what I feel

Won't turn it off
Don't think I can
It's part of life
It's who I am

It's brighter there
I'm better there
Words that float so pure and free
I can be who I want to be
In a sharp and shiny
Lit-up world
That made itself for me

My screen won't tell me
I'm too young
It reads my words
Hears what I've sung

Yeah, those strangers aren't my friends
Only care when my name trends
But there the party never ends
Never ends

It's brighter there
We're better there
Words that float so pure and free
I can be who I want to be
In a sharp and shiny
Lit-up world
That made itself for me

Yeah, tonight has been bizarre
Taking down a proper star
I guess maybe I've gone too far
Gone too far
But

It's brighter there
We're better there
Words that float so pure and free
I can be who I want to be
In a sharp and shiny
Lit-up world
That made itself for me.

CHAPTER TWELVE

'Katie.'

Someone was calling me. Amanda! Thank goodness. We were going to have the conversation we should have had last night.

'Mands?' I croaked.

'Katie.'

Amanda sounded different. Her voice was younger and higher. More like Lacey's.

'Katie.'

My bleary eyes tried to focus through a crust of sleep and yesterday's make-up. Manda was looking weirdly like Lacey too.

'Katie.'

Could it be possible that my sister had somehow morphed into my best friend?

'Wake up, KATIE.'

'Aaaaaaaaaaargh . . . Lace?!'

I sat up to find Lacey at the end of my bed. She was fully dressed, and she was looking rather worried.

'Are you OK?'

'I think so. Give me a sec.' I took a deep breath, and glanced around the room.

Little specks of dust danced in the sunlight. Clothes on the floor. My guitar in the corner. Amanda's perfectly made bed. Everything was where it normally would be. Except the person currently standing opposite me.

'Why are you here? It's Saturday morning. Shouldn't you be –' I tried to think what a normal person might do on a Saturday morning – 'asleep?'

'I got my brother to drive me over.'

'Wuh?' I know I sounded dense but it was still very early. Not even eleven o'clock.

Lacey opened a paper bag and thrust something sticky across the bed at me. An apple turnover. I ate a bit, and then the lot, and began to feel slightly more awake.

'Fanks, Lacey.'

I will say this for my BF. She may be a bit fickle when it comes to her choice of companions, but that girl knows how to brunch.

'No problem. Do you want another one? They were on three-for-two.'

'Split it?'

'OK.'

We had a quiet chew.

'Where's your sister?' said Lacey, looking over at her smooth navy duvet cover. Her drawers were closed, the wardrobe shut. It was as though last night's Jaz rampage had never happened.

'Gone to work, I suppose,' I said.

'How can you sleep through someone else getting up right next to you?'

Lacey, I should say, cannot sleep with even a bit of noise in her bedroom. I know this because when I stay over at hers, I can barely breathe without her complaining. That girl hears everything. Even the tiniest possible fart. Which I'd hardly noticed I'd done until she started to laugh.

'I'm great at not listening,' I said. 'It's my super skill. Just as well, given that we're having to share.'

'How's that going?'

'Not very well,' I admitted. 'Jaz was kind of winding her up last night. I'm finding that friendship a bit . . . difficult.'

'Then why did you invite her?' said Lacey.

'Because you were at Paige's,' I said, and we both went quiet.

'Um, yeah,' said Lacey. 'I came over to say sorry about that. It was, well, Paige was saying we had to go over all the pictures from the concert and I totally forgot about the dance party and . . .' She clocked that her apology wasn't going down ever so well and tailed off. 'And I know you're going through some stuff and I'm so . . . sorry.'

'S'OK,' I mumbled.

'Cool.'

I prised a bit of apple turnover from the roof of my mouth, and chewed, and thought about it. What, exactly, had I been so worked up about last night? In the Saturday-morning sunshine, with a nice breeze coming in from across the fields and the washing machine grumbling away downstairs, it was hard to remember.

'Hey, no school today,' I said, suddenly feeling incredibly happy. 'So are you sticking around? I should probably work on some stuff for my showcase thing. It would be nice to have some help.'

'Sure,' said Lacey. Then, 'Maybe have a shower, first.'

A few minutes later I staggered downstairs to find Adrian sitting at the kitchen table. He was kind of frowning at me. 'Morning.'

'Why aren't you at the shop?' Saturdays at Vox Vinyl are so busy that it takes both Adrian and Amanda to keep a handle on things.

'There's someone at the front door for you. A journalist.'

'What? Why? Aren't you going to let them in?'

'I thought we should have a chat first, make a plan . . . Katie, come back! Katie . . .'

I opened the door, and there, in the front garden, was a small man with brown hair, talking into his phone. When he saw me he hung up straight away, and gave me a smile so huge that I swear I caught a glimpse of his molars.

'Hi!'

'Hi,' I said. 'Can I help you?'

'I'm Chris. Chris Murrell. From NTV News. Don't suppose I can use your loo, can I?'

'Of course you can,' I said, showing him inside. 'It's in there. You have to flush it three times before it works, but that's normal. Have a good . . . one.'

'Thanks!'

I turned around to see Lacey and Adrian making huge, silent faces at me.

WHAT? I mimed.

Their mouths went very fast.

SLOW DOWN.

Their mouths went very fractionally slower.

The loo flushed three times.

Their mouths went extremely big and fast.

'Hi!' said Chris the journalist, coming out of the loo.

'Cup of tea, Chris?' said Adrian, managing to make those few words sound like he'd lost a battle.

'Love one,' said Chris, coming in and sitting down at the table like he was a Cox-kitchen regular. 'So Katie, love, love, love the new single.'

'Milk?' said Adrian, from over by the kettle. 'Sugar? And how did you get our address?'

'Milk, one sugar, thanks. Now, what made you write that wonderful song?'

'Oh. You really like it?'

Chris's eyes were gleaming. I have never seen anyone so awake before midday. 'I bloomin' *adore* it. You have a real talent for singing what the rest of us are thinking. It's going to be a smash.'

'Um.' I hadn't really thought of whether it would do well or not. But now that I did . . . 'Do you think so?'

'I know so,' said Chris. 'And how it came out, leaked

on the internet, and by Kurt from Karamel. Everyone's all over the backstory.'

'You certainly are,' said Lacey, helping herself to my secret stash of Coco Pops.

'I've never liked them,' I said. 'Boy band? More like boy bland.'

'Ha! Hahahahaha!' Chris bashed the table in appreciation, making the Coco Pops rattle. 'That's really clever!'

Finally.

'And this must be a big week for you, single out, first concert. How are you feeling?'

'Look, sorry, but no,' said Adrian, sitting down between us. 'We don't know who you are –'

'He's called Chris,' I said, helpfully.

'Or where you're from –'

'NTV news,' said Chris.

'You just show up on our doorstep, no explanation, and start questioning Katie and it's not on. Here's your tea. Milk, one sugar.'

'Great, thanks,' said Chris. 'Well, OK, I'm a journalist, as I said, and a huuuuge fan.'

'Thanks!'

'I'm just really excited about the next chapter of the whole Katie Cox saga.'

'How did you get our address?' said Adrian.

'And I thought I'd get a couple of quick comments ahead of what's going to be a major few days for you! So, this whole Karamel thing. I know where you're coming from. You've set up this battle, haven't you? Real music versus manufactured pap! The whole industry is starting to take notice.'

'No!'

'No,' said Lacey.

'Yes! And that online spat, last night, it was fan-tas-tic.'

'What online spat?' said Adrian.

'I was thinking I might go back and delete that,' I said.

Chris slammed his cup on to the table. 'Katie, you mustn't!'

'Mustn't I?'

'You know that your single's out the same day as Karamel's? We're thinking this could be a lead story. Battle of the bands!'

'Katie isn't a band,' said Lacey.

'What online spat?' said Adrian.

Chris was looking as excited as I'd ever seen a person. Certainly more excited than, say, my manager and my best friend, who were, respectively, drumming their meaty fingers on the table and letting my precious Coco Pops turn to brown gunge. If you're going to steal a person's Coco Pops, at least bother to eat them.

'So, what we're thinking is, we lead with your crusade to bring music back to its roots. No more team-written singles for manufactured bands. Get the industry back to homegrown, genuine talent. People with something to say. Never mind good looks and autotuned voices.'

'Katie looks OK,' said Lacey.

'That's not what he meant,' I told her, although a tiny part of me thought that perhaps it was.

'And so it's you in one corner, and your brilliant new song, and in the other, Karamel, with their overproduced single and stadium tour and T-shirts that cost forty pounds each, can you believe it?'

'Forty pounds! Who spends that much on a T-shirt?'

Lacey coughed. Then, when I looked at her, said, 'Savannah might have bought me one. Early birthday present.'

'But it wasn't your birthday. It was my birthday.'

'Have mine, if you want one that much.'

'I don't want one.'

'Then why are we—'

'You're the one who—'

'Ahem,' said Adrian.

We looked up to see that Chris was watching us. It occurred to me that I probably shouldn't have an argument with my bestie in front of a journalist. Even if I *was* right.

'So,' said Chris, as though he saw this kind of thing every day, 'we thought, we'll interview Kurt in the wings at your concert, you doing your thing in the background and then you'll come to his and we'll do the same. Show both interviews that night, talk about your singles, see who wins. It's just what we're looking for right now, all the right elements, youth, music, social media . . .'

'All right . . . I suppose . . .'

He stood up. 'So that's a yes? Brilliant!'

'NO.' Adrian rose to his feet like a kind of mountain, if a mountain can be wearing a Keane T-shirt and be in need of a shave. 'I don't know how you got our address. But the answer is no. All our press goes through Top Music, and I imagine they'll take a pretty dim view of this . . . this . . . media intrusion.'

I must say, it was quite impressive. Only, Chris didn't flinch. If anything, his smile got even brighter.

'Of course. Totally get that. But you know, it was Tony who gave me your address. Tony Topper? He loves the story. Even moved the single release dates around so that they'd coincide. He's one hundred and fifty per cent behind it.'

'You can't be more than one hundred per cent anything,' said Lacey, which was ironic, because I was pretty sure she was one hundred and fifty per cent against this.

'Katie's too young to get into some power play to sell singles,' said Adrian. 'I don't think Tony Topper has her best interests at heart.'

Chris's head jerked up. 'Really? Can I quote you on that?'

'No!'

'Now, look,' said Chris. 'Maybe he doesn't. And I know that you do. I respect that. Which is why I say, let's listen to Katie. Ask her what she wants.'

'I . . . I . . .' Adrian was clearly trying not to say that

he didn't care what I wanted.

'She's found her voice,' said Chris. 'Are we the ones to silence her?'

'Someone should,' murmured Lacey.

Thanks, Team Katie. Thanks a bunch. In fact . . .

'OK,' I said, first softly, then loudly. 'OK! I stand by what I said last night. Let's do it.'

'Lovely,' said Chris. 'I'll be in touch.'

'I'm calling Tony,' said Adrian.

Then we were back in the hall, and Chris was giving me a tiny salute, already on his phone as he stepped down into the front garden.

'She's a yes. Family's not keen, but . . .'

And he'd gone.

There was one of those silences where everyone is shouting stuff in their heads.

'What?' I said. 'Come on, spit it out.'

Adrian eyeballed me for a second. Then, 'I can't argue with you on this one, Katie. I don't like manufactured bands any more than you do. And I agree, the industry's over-commercialized.'

'But . . . ?' I said.

'But . . . this is a big deal. You're going out there, saying this stuff, a lot of people will get upset. And when people get upset, they get angry. And you're so young. You've got your whole life to tell the world what you think. I just reckon that maybe, this time, you should keep your thoughts to yourself.'

'So you're saying that because I'm young, my opinions don't count?'

'No, I'm not saying that.'

'Because that's what it sounds like.' Then . . . 'Dad would let me.'

I did know that this was the equivalent of pressing the big red button and there'd be all kinds of fallout. And I wasn't happy about it. I wasn't happy at all, especially when I saw Adrian's face.

But – NTV News! I mean, *come on*!

'I can't stop you,' said Adrian.

I looked over to Lacey, who shrugged.

'Great,' I said. And then, 'It's probably not that much of a story anyway.'

CHAPTER THIRTEEN

Adrian went off to the shop. Mum was at work, and Dad, who'd been out on a run, came in, took a long shower and then settled down on the sofa.

So Lace and I stayed up in my room and tried to work out a set list for the concert.

Which was, now I allowed myself to think about it, in four days' time.

Four days was quite soon.

Breathe breathe breathe.

'I'll start with "London Yeah",' I said. 'Because I'll be in London. That works, doesn't it? Or maybe I should do "Just Me".'

'Are you sure you don't want Savannah to dress you?' said Lacey. 'She's got these divine sparkly hot pants from her sister and they're way too big for her, massive, really, so we thought . . .'

'I'm sure.'

'Then what are you going to wear?'

'I don't know,' I said, in a way that was supposed to

indicate that the subject was closed.

'FYI, Savannah's really good at dressing people. Look at me! I look great today. And that's all Savannah. I didn't even have to buy anything new, she's genius with accessories.'

The annoying thing was that Lacey did look great. She had this striped blue-and-white cardie she always wears, but instead of shoving it over jeans, she'd put it over a strappy vest and mini skirt, and wrapped a skinny belt around it, which really showed off her waist and legs.

'Your belt is new,' I said.

'Sofie lent it to me. Those three have the most gorgeous stuff, really, you should see it. Paige has a walk-in wardrobe.'

'So, I'll start with "London Yeah". Then "Cake Boyfriend". Um, I might do "Spaghetti Hoops" – I know Tony's not keen, but I should do some new material . . . Then "Autocorrect", "That Belt", maybe the new one about my dad, "Just Me", and finish on "Can't Stand the Boy Band".'

'That was easy,' said Lacey, as her phone started to ring. 'Oh, hi, Sav. I'm with Katie. She seems fine. She doesn't want you to dress her. I know. I know! I tried my best.' She held the phone away from her face. 'Sav says at least don't wear your jeggings.'

'But I like my jeggings!'

She rolled her eyes and went back to her phone. 'Yes. No. No, we can't. I know, but a sample sale at Cindy's is not as important as Katie's concert. Yes, you are coming too.'

I opened my mouth to say that if Savannah would rather go to a Cindy's sample sale she was very much welcome, but Lacey was still talking.

'Supposing she has a meltdown mid-song? Or falls off the stage or something? This could be a complete disaster. Total public humiliation! You know what she's like. She needs her friends.' She hung up and smiled at me. 'OK, I've got you Savannah.'

'How generous.'

Was I supposed to be grateful for this sprinkling of Savannah stardust? Just a few of weeks ago, before the whole bedroom-recording-viral-music thing had happened, the Queen of Highlights, Princess of the Mani-Pedi and High Priestess of Juicy Couture had not counted Lacey and myself among her loyal subjects.

More importantly, neither of us had even cared.

Today, though . . .

'Katie?'

Dad was calling me from the sofa.

'What?'

'Come down! Now!'

Dad is not one of life's hurriers. This is a man who thinks that missing trains is not only normal, but inevitable.

By which I mean, if he says come now, you come.

'What?' I hurtled into the lounge with Lacey, forgetting that the door had recently fallen off and we had to be delicate with it now. It fell off.

'. . . Katie Cox, with her new single "Can't Stand the Boy Band" is unrepentant. The young singer-songwriter . . .'

'That's you!' said Dad.

'That's me! And that's the man from this morning. He was in the kitchen, like, two hours ago.'

'And he's talking about you!'

'Shh!' said Lacey.

'. . . said on social media last night that Karamel are the enemy of good music, accusing them of playing songs written in boardrooms by middle-aged men.'

143

'You tell 'em, Katie!' said Dad.

'Shhh!' said Lacey.

'Karamel have hit back, releasing a statement saying that they either write or co-write all their songs themselves, and that they have the utmost respect for their fans.

'Head of Top Music, Tony Topper, spoke to NTV this morning, saying that both acts are releasing singles on the same day.'

'That's him,' I said. 'That's Tony.' He was standing there in an expensive-looking simple white T-shirt showing just a curl or two of chest hair at the neck, looking as relaxed as if he was watching the telly, not on it.

'Shhh!' said Lacey.

'All I can say is that I respect them both. They're making great music. But the question for viewers is – are you Team Katie or Team Karamel?'

The screen cut back to Chris, smiling into the camera.

'The UK's most established act is up against one of its most exciting newcomers. It's the biggest chart battle in years, and so far, at least, this result is too close to call.'

'That Tony's a genius,' said Dad. 'An absolute genius.'

'He kind of is,' I said. 'I mean, I thought he was down on me because I wouldn't play one of his rubbishy songs. I assumed he'd given up on me. But this is . . . I mean, this is huge!'

'Yeah,' said Lacey.

'So, how's that set list coming along?' Dad grinned. 'All eyes are going to be on you, my girl.'

All the eyes? 'Uh, it's OK.'

'Not feeling too nervous, I hope?'

'. . . No.'

'Great! This is such an opportunity.' He beamed. 'My little princess, all grown up, out there, in the spotlight . . .'

'The thing is,' I said, because his words were making my stomach do worrying things, 'it's actually a very intimate concert. Low key. Tony and I agreed that we'd start small.'

'Doesn't look small from where I'm sitting,' said Dad.

'Very small,' I said, mainly to myself. 'Small, and intimate and low key.'

I turned down Savannah's offer of that pink limo to take me to the gig, and in the end, it was Adrian who drove us there, four sleepless nights later, to a soundtrack of the Pet Shop Boys and early Pulp.

It wasn't the most fun of journeys. For my part, I was playing songs over and over in my head, until none of them made sense any more and I'd completely forgotten why I'd written them. Meanwhile Adrian was mainly swearing, at the traffic, at other drivers and at the lack of decent signposting on the M25. So much so that I hardly registered when he started banging his fist against the steering wheel.

'Ach.'

'What is it?' said Amanda.

'See for yourself,' said Adrian.

The road outside the venue had been blocked off by some kind of demonstration. A hundred or possibly two hundred people were standing around doing demo-type things like holding hands and chanting and waving flappy homemade signs.

'Why are they doing it here?' I said. 'There's all of London to stand and shout in, after all.'

'I hadn't heard anyone was marching today,' said Mum.

'This isn't an ordinary demo,' said Adrian. 'They're too young.'

Now he came to mention it, they were all around my age, or younger, wearing T-shirts and hoodies and little tiny skirts, with fluffed-up hair and angry faces.

'They're . . .' Adrian stopped. 'Ah. I wondered if this might happen.'

It was then that I read the nearest sign. It said:

KATIE COX IS A WITCH

Which made me read the other signs. I got:

KARAMEL FOREVER

and

BAD APPLE

and

KATIE HATER

and

UGLY FACE UGLY SOUL

And then I decided I would stop reading the signs.

'I'm sorry, what's going on?' asked Mum, who really needed to get with the programme.

'They're Karamel fans,' said Amanda. 'And I think they're a bit upset with Katie.'

'I am not a hater,' I said. 'I just happen to be giving my opinion about something, which is that I hate it.'

'Talking of which,' said Adrian, 'K, maybe you want to turn away from the window?'

Given the view, this was not a difficult decision to make.

'Yeah. Let's make it into the venue alive,' said Amanda, which I think we all felt was unnecessary.

Thank the Lord I hadn't gone for the Savannah-mobile. Adrian's car was old and dented and smelt of fags and mints, but it was, at least, reasonably anonymous.

Shame I couldn't stay in it forever, really.

'All right?' A bloke with an earpiece was talking to Adrian through the window. 'Round the back. Don't worry, it's ticket holders only.'

So Adrian attempted a three-point turn, which quickly became a twenty-seven-point turn, as all the while I tried to tune out the chanting, and Mum, who kept saying:

'Why do you always have to upset people, Katie?'

'I'm just saying my opinion.'

'Yes, but you're famous now. Your opinions matter.'

'And they didn't before?!'

Mum's fingers began to massage the bit between her nose and her forehead.

Then I was safely lodged in a dressing room with 'Katie Cox' taped to the door. Only it wasn't safe, not safe at all, because in half an hour I would be onstage performing in front of two hundred and fifty people.

My brain took in the office chairs, the bunch of flowers with a note from Top Music, the two bottles of mineral water, one fizzy and one still, anything to distract me from the fact that in half an hour I would be onstage performing to two hundred and fifty people.

'I can't believe that in just half an hour you'll be onstage performing to two hundred and fifty people!'

said Lacey, who *had* travelled in the Savannah-mobile.

'That's so many people,' said Paige.

'And you haven't even done your make-up,' said Savannah.

'Yes I have,' I said.

'Oh,' said Savannah.

With eleven of us in the room, plus my guitar, it was starting to feel a tad claustrophobic.

'Can I get you anything?' said Adrian.

'A drink would be great,' said Dad.

'And for me,' said Jaz. I have no idea how she'd got there.

'I meant Katie,' said Adrian.

'I'm fine, thanks,' I said.

The walls, which were a very deep green, seemed to be closing in on me, like I was being suffocated by spinach. I shut my eyes.

'Katie.' Amanda's voice sounded far away. 'Are you OK?'

'Fine,' I said, opening my eyes to see Lacey looking down the scrawled bit of paper that was my set list.

'You're going to play "Can't Stand the Boy Band"?'

'Yes,' I said.

'Even though you know how much it upset all those Karamel fans?'

'Um . . .' I said, because she was maybe perhaps a little bit right. I mean, I'd known that my song would annoy people, but not so much that they felt like they had to make signs and come to my gig to protest . . . This was a bad idea.

Not just the song, not just the chart battle, but this concert.

Everything.

All of it.

Dad was strumming on my guitar, while Savannah was demonstrating to Paige the perfect way to use lip liner, using Sofie's mouth as a canvas. I sank down into a chair and put my head between my knees.

Then: 'Right, that's it. Everyone out.'

'What?'

'You don't mean me,' said Savannah.

'I do,' said Adrian. 'I'm Katie's manager and I want this room clear in the next thirty seconds. Go find a place to watch. Or get a drink. I don't care. But GO.' He caught my shoulder as I made for the door. 'Not you, bozo.'

'Oh.' I looked back at the room, which was now

wonderfully empty. 'Hey, thank you.'

'I'll call you when it's time,' said Adrian.

Ten minutes to go.

I tuned my guitar, and then retuned it. I sang a few notes into the mirror, which had lights all the way around it, and reapplied my eyeliner.

Five minutes to go.

Don't be sick, don't be sick.

Then I went into the toilet and was sick.

There was a gentle knock on the door.

'Katie?'

'Yeah.'

'You're on.'

CHAPTER FOURTEEN

There was a thick darkness to the wings. Deep and thick and I was in the middle, down deep, in the depths of my personal grave.

Very, very close, I could hear them, the audience, the two hundred and fifty people who were about to see me completely fall apart.

Someone tapped me on the shoulder. 'Katie, hi!'

'Yaaaaaaargh!'

I must have jumped about ten metres into the air.

'Sorry, Katie, it's Chris. From NTV news. You remember?'

'Oh, right. Hi, Chris.' I'm not the world's greatest conversationalist at the best of times, and this definitely wasn't the best of times.

'You remember the deal? We're just going to have a quick chat with Kurt while you're singing; he'll be here in a minute. If we can get the VT edited in time we're looking at a slot on tomorrow's ten o'clock news. Have a great show!'

And before I had time to think, or even breathe, the

 153

lights started doing some crazy whizzing about, and this huge voice came down from the sky, or possibly the speakers, and Kurt and Chris stopped mattering because I knew I was going to have to sing.

'Ladies and gentlemen . . .'

I don't want to be here.

'She's a rising star. Our youngest, freshest, realest talent . . .'

Please, let me be somewhere else.

'Give a very warm welcome to . . .'

Anywhere else.

'KATIE COX!'

I hesitated. And then, on legs that felt like they were someone else's, stepped out, from the darkness, into bright, bright light.

It was like when you do a somersault in the swimming pool and halfway through forget which way is up. For a long second I couldn't see anything, couldn't hear anything, and then, slowly, the world settled.

They were there, just beyond the end of the stage. A blur, face melting into face, shifting, coughing. I could smell their hot breath.

Through the murmuring, a single, lonely *whoop*.

'Um,' I said, sliding into place on to a chair and trying to tilt the microphone so that it was nearer my mouth. It wouldn't move. I tried harder.

It wouldn't budge and wouldn't budge and I was seriously considering giving it a bash with my guitar when it occurred to me that I could just move a bit further forward. So I did that.

'Hi.'

The front row began to focus. Lacey, next to Amanda. Jaz. Nicole. Savannah, Paige and Sofie. Tony. Mum. Dad.

They seemed . . . excited.

And then, less excited.

The more I stared into the audience, the more they shuffled and looked away. As though until two minutes ago they had really been worked up about seeing me in the flesh. But now I was here, my flesh pale and sweaty and trembling, everyone was starting to think it might have been better to have stayed home.

I know I was.

'So I'm Katie Cox. As in the apple. Not that there's an apple called Katie, but maybe there should be! Ha ha.'

I swear I heard Jaz sigh.

'So, yes. Katie Cox. That's me.'

I glanced sideways. The darkness was only three steps away. Two steps, if I made them big ones. I could be off the stage and out the back door in, what, a minute, maybe a minute and a half?

In fact, I was just wondering exactly how much money I'd owe Tony if I ran out now when I noticed that I was somehow still talking.

Isn't it amazing what the human body can do?

'So. Anyway. I'm going to p-play you a couple of songs. More than a couple. Some songs. Of mine. That I wrote.'

With the most massive effort that anyone has ever made, I managed to lift up my guitar and get my numb fingers into position on the strings.

'This one's called "London Yeah". Because we're in London. Um, yeah. Yeah! Yeah.'

I strummed the opening chords.

Trafalgar Square and then Big Ben
Bond Street and Covent Garden
Greenwich and the Cutty Sark
And a really massively big Primark

Put your hands in the air
For London yeah

This was OK. I sounded a bit wavery, but it wasn't too bad.

 Camden Town and Kensington
Notting Hill and . . .

And . . . where?

I'd forgotten the next line.

In a fraction of a zillionth of a millisecond I raced to
the bit of my brain where I kept all my lyrics, and . . .

Nothing. Completely empty.

Like a cathedral, if someone had taken all the seats
and altar out, and switched the lights off. And maybe,
right in the middle, left a tiny bit of paper that said 'sorry'.

Camden Town and Kensington
Notting Hill and . . . Aberdeen

Where had I got *that* from? Aberdeen isn't in London. Not
even slightly.

But it did fit, sort of. And is, at least, a place.

Greenwich and the Cutty Sark
And a really massively big Primark

Put your hands in the air
For London yeah.

No one put their hands in the air, either for London, or for me. I got to the end of the song, and there was an embarrassed pause, then a dribble of applause.

Just the whole rest of the concert to go.

'OK, cool, thanks. This next one is called "Cake Boyfriend". I wrote it because my friend Savannah, she's here, in the front row, hey Savannah –' Savannah quietly pulled her jacket over her head – 'she had this massive cake at her party and she loved it so much it was almost like a boyfriend and I thought wouldn't it be great to have a cake that was a boyfriend. Anyway.'

Pat-a-cake
Pat-a-cake
Baker's man
Bake me a boy as fast as you can

Give him fudge for hair
And frosted blue eyes
And finish him off with

TWANGGGGGG . . .

I'd snapped a string.

'What is wrong with me?' I murmured, or rather, meant to murmur, only the microphone picked it up and made it really loud.

Adrian appeared at my side and took the guitar as I stood, now shaking, and the audience began to whisper and rustle.

And I thought, *I won't even have nightmares any more. Not now. There won't be any point.*

Adrian handed back my guitar and I strummed again.

Out of tune.

Now the murmurs were getting restless. In fact, some of them had stopped being murmurs and become proper conversations. Probably about me being completely terrible.

Words floated up in front of my eyes, words from those signs, just outside.

KATIE COX IS A WITCH.

BAD APPLE.

UGLY FACE UGLY SOUL

They were right, of course. I was useless and ugly and wrong. The people outside knew it. Everyone inside knew it, too. I should get off the stage now, crawl back under my rock and stay there forever.

'This is going really badly, isn't it?' I said, more to myself than anyone else.

There was this HUGE laugh.

And I began to play.

Pat-a-cake
Pat-a-cake
Baker's man
Bake me a boy as fast as you can

This time, it was better. I even started to feel it, a bit, towards the end, so, as it finished, I played straight through the applause, on into 'Autocorrect', then 'That Belt'.

That belt
That belt

That turquoise belt
With sparkly stones and bits of felt

From the back, people were joining in.

Six ninety-nine
And it could have been mine
With sparkly stones and bits of felt

My fingers were behaving. My voice seemed to know what to do. The singing from the audience got louder, and I could hear Adrian, and Mum, and Dad.

I was . . . I was almost starting to enjoy it.

My dad rocks hard
My dad is ace
My dad plays lead guitar
And drums and sax and bass

My dad's way cool
My dad's so fine
My dad lives his dreams
And shows me mine

Now the audience wasn't this frightening thing any more. It was more like a wave, or a huge blob of power, and I was riding it, or feeding from it or something, because the more it cheered and stamped, the better I felt. Especially when I went into 'Just Me' and everyone held up their phones and swayed.

Then, it was finished, and . . .

'So, this is the last song,' I said. 'I know it's been a bit, erm, controversial. But hey. It's something I really believe.'

I picked out the first few notes.

Can't stand the boy band . . .

And – I'm not kidding – the room went *crazy*.

They knew all the words, every last one, and they half sang them, half shouted them along with me.

Plastic faces, stupid hair
Can't stand the boy band
The matching clothes they wear

While most of me was there, in the room, a small part of

me was saying to Tony, *See? We're not stupid. We are not soppy idiots, ready to be fed your mushy pap.*

The tattooed Chinese symbols
On the skin that's perma-tanned
I can't stand the boy band

Louder.

Don't like the boy band
Singing songs about their nans
Don't like the boy band
Hanging round their camper vans

Their lyrics are predictable
Their music's oh so bland
I don't like the boy band

I want to be *here*, I thought.

Oh poor sweet boy band
Your music makes me heave

Exactly here, exactly now.

You poor sad boy band
Soon one of you will leave

Forever.

And if you think you'll be remembered
Then you misunderstand
RIP the boy band.

I couldn't stop. They wouldn't stop. We roared it, again
and again and again.

Can't . . . stand . . . the . . . boy band
Can't . . . stand . . . the . . . boy band
Can't . . . stand . . . the . . . boy band

And as they chanted, I pulled the microphone up, and it
came away from the stand so easily, and I shouted,

'This is for real music! No more manufactured rubbish!
No more overproduced tracks, no more autotuning! No!
More! Boy bands!'

A spotlight swung across the audience. As the beam swept through I saw that everyone was cheering. Except... the light caught a face. Lacey. She was watching me with eyes that burned.

'No more boy bands,' I said. And then, finally, I let my guitar drop.

'Thanks very much. Goodnight!'

CHAPTER FIFTEEN

With one leap I was in the wings. Wings?! It was like I *had* wings. It's such a massive cliché, but really, I was bouncing, floating, a sort of human hoverboard, surfing high on the applause, hugging my guitar to me, feeling like Christmas morning and the end of exams and glittering swimming pools under summer skies, only a million, billion times better.

'That was brilliant!'

'Oh my God, thanks!' I panted at the darkened face, which smiled and moved out into the light and became . . .

Kurt.

Kurt from Karamel.

If I'd been a hoverboard, I would have run out of batteries. As it was, I sort of went, 'Uhhhh.'

He was younger than I'd thought. No, that wasn't it. I hadn't really thought of him being any age, because in my head, he hadn't had an age, because of not being a proper person.

Now, though, I saw that he wasn't much older than me, and not hugely taller, either. He was much better looking than me, though, like his eyes and nose and mouth were all fighting to be the best thing on his face. Of course, it didn't help that *my* eyes were still funny from the spotlights, so one second I was looking at his nose and then it turned into this swimmy burst of yellow, and then back into a nose.

'I'm not saying I loved the last number. But the rest was great. I can't believe that's only the second time you've played live. I was puking from nerves for at least my first twenty gigs.'

'Actually,' I said, my voice far steadier than my legs, which were wibbling all over the place, 'I did puke. Before I went on. You can't smell it, can you?'

'No.'

'Phew.'

We stood there, listening to the cheers turn to claps to the sound of people picking up their jackets and stuff, and I tried to process the fact that I'd just led two hundred and fifty people in an anthem against Kurt from Karamel and then asked him whether or not I smelt of sick.

'So, look,' said Kurt, 'I've got to go, my car's here. But

 167

see you tomorrow night, yeah?'

I gaped at him, feeling as stupid as I've ever felt, which, let me tell you, is really quite stupid. 'What's happening tomorrow night?'

'Your turn,' said Chris, who was also still there, as it turned out. 'We interviewed Kurt when you were doing all your "I hate boy bands" business. Such a great visual. And then we'll do your interview while he's singing his single. Tomorrow night at the O2.'

'Right, yes. Um, see you tomorrow. And – oh, Tony! Hi!'

Tony Topper had his hand on my elbow, guiding me towards a different door, leaving Chris and Kurt to melt into the darkness. 'Come on through, come on through.'

'To where?' I was still holding my guitar.

'Your party,' said Tony. 'Nothing big, just a few people from Top Music, bit of press, the guest list . . .'

We went through a heavy door, straight past a woman with a clipboard, and into a room that was completely full of people.

And – oooh. I put my guitar down. Because there was a waiter, with a tray. Of *things*.

'Can I?' My stomach was feeling very empty.

'Sure.' Then Tony saw that I'd taken three chickensatay sticks. 'Although we really must have that chat about a personal trainer.'

'KA-AA-T-IEEE!' Paige came exploding in like she'd been fired from a cannon. 'You were AM-AAAA-ZING!'

'You were pretty good,' said Savannah, just behind her. 'Except at the beginning, which was ropey, babes. You need to work on that.'

'Um, thanks,' I said.

'And –' Savannah stopped, and wrinkled her nose. 'Can you smell sick? I can smell sick.'

Then, thank goodness, Mands and Mum were racing across the room.

'You were brilliant!'

'So amazing.'

I glowed. I actually glowed.

'Although –' Mum had her hand on my arm – 'the song about your father . . .'

'I'll write one about you too,' I said. 'For the album. It's only fair.'

'That's not what I . . .' She sighed. 'And . . . I just . . . Do you have to be so *angry*, Katie?' She looked out across the party. 'Everyone was so angry.'

'It's just a genuine expression of my dislike of the

way the music industry is going,' I told her. 'What used to be real has become a corporate machine designed to manipulate young people and I want to bring things back to the music. Enough greed . . .' I tailed off. 'Are those *tiny Yorkshire puddings*?'

Mum didn't look especially convinced. 'You sounded great, but all this rage, it's not you. And if you say things like that, you're giving the other side a licence to hate you.'

'Then let them,' I said. 'I can handle it.'

She pulled me into a sudden hug. 'But you're still my little girl.'

'I AM NOT.' I decided to focus on the important bit of the conversation, which was that I'd sounded good. If Mum couldn't handle my impending adulthood, that was her problem.

Sofie was taking selfies with pretty much everyone in the room. Savannah was messaging frantically, while Nicole and Jaz were throwing miniature samosas off the balcony. And Lacey . . .

'Hey, BF,' I said, to the lone figure lurking by the coats.

'Oh.' Lacey looked up and attempted a smile. 'Hey! Well done.'

'Thanks. Did you have fun?'

'Yeah. Thanks for inviting me. I mean, I still don't like that last song. And the one about your dad was a bit full on. But the rest was ace.'

'OK, well, we can agree to disagree, right?'

'I suppose,' she said. 'Ooh, are those mini pizzas?'

'Pesto flatbreads,' I told her. 'Go get 'em, girlfriend.'

I stood, and watched, feeling weirdly outside of everything, seeing as how it was supposed to be for me. Flat. Flat as a pesto flatbread.

'Oi! Princess! Over here!' Dad's arm wove around my back. 'You rocked my world tonight.'

'I did?'

'So hard. You are a great talent, my girl.'

'I am?'

'Those lyrics! That tune!' He swiped up my guitar and began to strum 'My Dad'. 'Phenomenal.'

The people nearest us were beginning to turn around, and for a second, I started to feel embarrassed. Only then, as Dad's fingers rippled up and down the strings, and everyone started to smile, and tap their feet, I remembered.

This was Dad.

And when Dad plays, it's like your ears are filling with sunshine.

A circle was forming around him, so I moved back and out of the way.

'Well now.' It was Tony. 'It seems you have tapped into something, Katie. I'm not often proved wrong. But this time . . .'

'So I'm forgiven?'

'Make the top ten and you're completely forgiven.' He laughed.

'When does it go on sale?'

'Midnight tonight. And . . . you're sure? You don't want any production on it whatsoever? Because we can ramp up the bass, smooth over the vocals, no one ever need know.'

'Absolutely not,' I said. 'I mean, that's the whole point, isn't it? I want the sound raw. Unmixed. Real. True.'

'True,' repeated Tony. 'Maybe that can be the name of your album?'

'Yes!' I said. 'I like that. *Katie Cox: True.* You're really good at this!'

'I know,' said Tony.

Dad looked up from his guitar and gave us a wink.

'I've had a few emails from him,' said Tony. 'More than a few.'

'Oh, yes,' I said. 'He wanted to send you his demo.'

'And he did,' said Tony. 'Several versions.' We listened for maybe twenty seconds, as Dad slid from 'Hotel California' into a jazz version of 'Sweet Child o' Mine'. 'The surprise is, he's good.'

I had this moment of relief, which turned into a thud of guilt. What had I been expecting? Dad was a professional. Too much time around Amanda, that's what it was. 'Of course he's good!'

'Have you heard of Papaya?' said Tony. 'She's fresh from kids' TV, making her first album. I could put him on it.'

'Could you? That would be fantastic,' I said. 'I know he's looking for work at the moment. When would he start?'

'Recording's in a few weeks' time. Nice little studio in West Hollywood. I'll get the contract over . . .'

Dad was beaming as his hands danced an impossible dance across the frets, and I remembered the feeling of finding him on the doorstep, the smell of him, how he'd held me, tight, against his jacket. And how far away Hollywood was. How very far away.

The party seemed to freeze, as though we were in a

film or something, and in my head, I walked over and looked Dad in the eyes, and tried to say goodbye again. Had a proper, honest go at sending him back to California and Catriona mark II, whoever she might be. Soon I'd stop remembering quite how his face moved, let alone the way he'd grab me for a sudden hug, or . . .

'I'm not sure it's a good idea, actually,' I said. 'Dad's had a few problems.'

Not what Tony was expecting. 'What kind of problems?'

'Oh, you know,' I said, lightly. 'Personality problems. It's kind of well known that he's a bit . . . unreliable. You'll be expecting him in the studio, and instead he's off on a plane to the other side of the world, without even –' I caught myself; where had *that* come from?

'I'm glad you told me,' said Tony. 'Papaya's a busy girl. She can't wait around for some no-show guitarist.'

'Better that you know now,' I said, bagging another satay stick from a passing waiter, as Tony drifted away.

The waiter didn't move, though, so I took another stick, and then another, swallowing hard down a throat that had gone painful and dry.

Anything to keep Dad here.

Anything.

CHAPTER SIXTEEN

It's good to know what your strengths are. My particular strengths, in no particular order, are:

- pizza (eating, not making)
- music (making, not eating)
- sleep.

The morning after the concert, I was really giving it some on that last one. In fact, I only woke when a pair of knickers hit me in the face.

'Murhph?' I removed them, and opened my eyes. 'Urgh! Manda, your pants went in my *mouth*!'

'Calm down,' said Mands. 'They're clean.'

I sat up to see that every inch of the room was covered in her clothes. And her phone was blasting out Alanis Morissette.

Seriously. When it comes to sleeping through things, I'm the bomb.

'Rise and shine, superstar.'

'Isn't it Thursday? Why are you not at work?'

'Day off,' said Amanda. 'I'm having a clear-out.' Alanis finished and her phone started playing something by a very famous band who I am not allowed to name. 'Hey, Dad's on this.'

'IS he? I thought they did all their own guitar.'

'So did Dad. Apparently not.'

We stopped and listened for a bit. Now that she'd told me, it was completely obvious that Dad was playing. The notes were sliding up and up, more like a voice than an instrument. Dad can make a guitar sing.

'It's been funny, having him back again,' said Mands, holding a navy top up against her chest. 'There's loads of stuff I'd forgotten that he did.'

'Like what?' I asked.

'Like that dee-dah tune he hums in the shower. The same one, every morning.'

'Oh, yeah!'

'And –' Amanda chucked the top into a pile and reached for a floppy cardie – 'that jangly thing he does with his pockets. Or how his socks never match. I wonder what else I'll forget?'

'Why would you forget anything else? He's not going anywhere.'

'Not now, but –' she set the cardie down on to the bed, smoothing down the arms as though it was a frightened animal – 'you know he can't stay forever, don't you?'

'I don't see why not,' I said. 'I don't mind giving up the den. We never go in there.'

'It's not good for Mum and Adrian,' said Amanda. 'And . . . it's not good for us.'

'Speak for yourself!'

Amanda did that thing she does where she goes from being this cool friend-type person who happens to look a lot like I do, to becoming a kind of cross between a headmistress and the Queen. 'Katie. Listen to me, because I know you. And I get that you and Dad are close. But the way you are when he's around, that song you did last night, it's like you're in love or something.'

'You're saying you don't love Dad?!'

'Of course I'm not saying that. All right, not in love, but you go all starry-eyed and it's like you can't see when he behaves in a way that is completely unreasonable.'

'Like how?'

'Um, OK. So, for example, Mum and Ade are pretty

hard up right now but Dad's not offered them a penny.'

'He's broke. He spent everything he had renting the dolphin flat and—'

'Exactly! He frittered his cash away renting somewhere totally unsuitable and now he's back and on the scrounge! You have to tell him to go home, Katie. He listens to you.'

'This *is* home.' I got up and made for the door. There's only so much a girl can take before breakfast.

'It's your home. It's not his home.'

I was almost out of there, but I paused in the doorway, just long enough to say, 'It's our home. And he's our dad.'

Me, Lacey and Mad Jaz had parked ourselves on our special bit of grass behind the labs. Lace had her legs stretched out in front of her, attempting to get a bit of a tan. Jaz was sitting in the shade. Sometimes I think Jaz carries the shadows around with her, the way other people might have a big handbag, or BO.

'What was your favourite thing about last night?' said Lacey. 'If you had to choose one thing.'

'The bit where I pinged Amanda's bra strap,' said Jaz.

'You pinged Amanda's bra?' Manda–Jaz relations were bad enough already. 'What, are you seven or something?'

'Yeah,' said Jaz, looking very pleased with herself.

'I liked it when you got into the music and stopped shaking,' said Lacey. 'Until then I was worried you were going to puke.'

'That was a good bit,' I agreed, feeling my phone buzz in my pocket.

A text.

Can't wait for the interview tonight. Car will pick you up at 5.30 and take you straight to concert. Ten o'clock news here we come! Chris

Oh, yes. That. The Karamel concert. It might be nice to bring a bit of moral support. Even if the support thought that I was without morals.

I glanced over to Lace and opened my mouth. Only, Jaz spoke first.

'So, when's it out?'

'The single? It's out now.'

'I might get it later,' said Jaz.

Now, Jaz isn't one of the world's greatest shoppers. By which I mean, she's great at choosing stuff, but she seems to have a bit of a block on the paying part of the process. So the idea of her parting with proper cash was really quite exciting.

'If you buy it on CD then I'll sign it,' I said. 'Vox Vinyl's got loads. What about you, Lace?'

'Join the dark side,' said Jaz.

'So,' said Lacey, in what was the most obvious change of subject in the whole history of changing subjects. 'Are you going to ask Dominic Preston out, then?'

'Why would I do that?'

'Because of being in love with him.'

'I am not in love with him,' I said, making our private motion for shutting up at her, because my love life (or lack of it) wasn't something I much fancied getting into around the madness that was Jaz.

'You said you really liked him,' said Lacey. 'And he seems to like you, and the disco is next week. So, ask him out!'

'Only if you ask someone out too.'

'Like who?'

'Um . . . Devi Lester?' I suggested.

'Katie, I don't have to go out with someone just because you are. We are different people.'

'But I'm not going out with anyone,' I said, trying to

picture asking Dominic Preston out, and finding it very, very easy to imagine him saying a big fat no. 'I'm . . . I'm too busy with my music right now. You know. Writing my album. Also, it's not like I need a man to give my life meaning.' It occurred to me that it would be good if Lace had a boyfriend; if nothing else it would take the heat off me. 'But you should totally get together with Devi.'

'So *I* should go out with someone because my life is so very empty and meaningless,' said Lacey. 'Thanks, Katie.'

Which was not what I meant at all, and she knew it. And I knew she knew it. And she knew that I knew she knew it.

'I'd better go,' I said. 'Need to get my stuff sorted out so I can make a quick getaway after school.'

'Why?'

'Because,' I said, as pointedly as I could, 'I've got to go all the way to the O2 for a Karamel concert, just to do a stupid annoying interview. Total waste of an evening. Laters.'

'Katie, there's a big silver car outside. Apparently it's for you.'

Mum did not sound impressed.

'Oh, that,' I said, peering out the window. 'Yes, that's for me.'

Which is when I remembered that I hadn't especially told her about the whole *News at Ten* shebang.

'You do not have my permission to go out unaccompanied on a school night. And—'

'HEY! KATIE!' It was Dad, waving both arms.

I made for the front door, Mum just behind me.

Dad was standing on the drive, next to a confused-looking bloke in a suit.

'Sorry, what's going on?'

'I'm supposed to be driving a Katie Cox to the O2,' said suit bloke.

'Oh, are you?' said Mum.

'Er . . . yes . . . ?'

'Katie, we seem to be having some fairly serious communication issues. You were out last night, fine, OK, that was a special occasion, but there is no need for you to go gallivanting off again this evening.'

I wasn't totally sure what 'gallivanting' meant, but I could tell it wasn't good.

'It's a press thing,' I said, trying to sound as reasonable and mature as I could. 'For the single.'

'In what way is going to the O2 related to your single?'

'Well, I'm going to be interviewed while Karamel are singing and I'm going to say how I think they are destroying music. It's going to be on the ten o'clock news!'

Mum was getting less impressed by the second. And she hadn't been impressed to start with. 'If you'd told me in advance I might have said yes. But you didn't. So the answer is no.'

The bloke in the suit looked awkward. 'Can't take you without parental permission,' he said.

'That's all right, I'm her dad. Of course she's going!'

'Benjamin . . .'

'Er, Dad . . .'

'What?' Dad was practically dancing on the spot. 'He's chauffeuring you to a concert! Take a tip from your old dad, Katie – never turn down a freebie.'

'Katie is in deep water, Benjamin; you saw what it was like last night, she needs to take a step back and—'

'Last night was a huge success!' said Dad.

'Last night was terrifying,' said Mum.

He put his hand on her arm, and I saw her try not to flinch. 'Zoe, love, you're not a creative person; you can't be expected to understand. But I'm like Katie; I get it. I'm with her on this. And I'll look after her.'

Mum was looking distinctly unhappy. 'I don't want her going off into the middle of goodness knows where all on her own . . .'

Now, I have to say, in the interests of family harmony, I was beginning to think that I might leave it. Some things are worth a bit of screaming, but a Karamel concert isn't exactly one of them. Plus, despite my epic sleep, I was sort of feeling a bit tired; I reckon even Beyoncé couldn't deal with a concert followed by a full day of school. An early night and a happy mother – it was an appealing combination.

'Then I'll go with her,' said Dad. 'It would be nice to have a bit of time just the two of us.'

'Really? Because—'

'Come on, Katie,' he said, looking up from inside the car, where he'd already sat down and – blimey – even taken off his shoes.

I ducked my head, but Mum still managed to catch my eye, and held it, steady and unhappy, and there was that pulling sensation that I hated so much, more than anything.

Would it never go away, that feeling, that I'd had for

years and years, every time they argued, and in those still, cold hours after the shouting had finished and Dad was 'having a lie-down' or Mum was just 'going for a drive' where I was stretching in two directions at once, tighter and tighter and tighter, and I knew if I made even the smallest movement I would tear apart – would it never let me be?

'You coming, princess?'

A whole evening with Dad, though.

'I'll see you later,' I told Mum, climbing in beside him.

Her mouth opened wide, but then we were off down the drive, leaving her, and whatever it was that she was shouting, behind.

'This is fun, isn't it?'

I looked up to see Dad pouring himself a glass of something from a mini fridge.

'Um, yeah.'

'I could get used to this.' He downed his drink and poured out another. 'Want something?'

I lifted up what turned out to be a bottle of pear cider.

'I don't think so,' said Dad, nudging it away. 'Hey, someone has to be responsible here.'

'I wasn't going to have any. I was just seeing what it was.'

'Of course you were,' said Dad, opening up a little bag of peanuts he'd got from somewhere. 'How about one of these? They're wasabi flavour!'

I took one, before remembering that wasabi is basically mustard, which is basically disgusting.

'Hey, that Tony's not the easiest chap to get hold of, is he?'

'Oh,' I said, making sure to face out the window so he couldn't see my cheeks flame, 'Tony's very busy. But I'm sure he'll come back to you. Be patient.'

'Of course, of course,' said Dad. 'And it's nice to have a bit of a holiday. Spend some time with my girls.'

Just to get it done, so that Mands would let it drop and we could all get on with our lives, I took a deep breath and then another one, and said, 'Do you think it's OK for you to be staying so long?'

'Yeah, yeah,' he said. 'It's fine! I mean, I know your mother is a bit uptight. And that Adrian, he's, well, he's not exactly . . . but they don't mind really. They'd have said!'

'That's what I thought.'

No, Katie, do it properly.

'But, Manda, she reckons it might be good for you to . . .'
No, I couldn't tell him to move out, I just couldn't. In the
last second, I switched the words: '. . . pay a bit of rent.'

'Ah, Miss Sensible,' said Dad. 'She'll go far.'

I wasn't sure what to say to that.

'Thing is,' said Dad, 'I haven't got much. In the way of
money.'

'I thought you were majorly busy? That everyone
wanted you?'

'I am,' said Dad. 'Just . . . not . . . currently.'

'But, haven't you got loads of savings?'

'Not . . . really.'

This didn't seem quite right. Because the one thing
we'd heard during the divorce, and after the divorce,
and in the weeks leading up to the divorce, was how Dad
was, in Mum's words, 'swanning off with half a house in
his back pocket'. Mum wouldn't lie. Surely, she wouldn't.
Only, Dad wouldn't either.

'I don't understand,' I said slowly. 'I thought . . . the
settlement . . .'

'It was a great apartment,' said Dad, and from the
look on his face, part of him was still there. 'Dolphins!

From the kitchen window! And I was busy. Busy enough to justify it at the time . . . only, not quite busy enough. And Catriona needed money. For—'

'Her Pilates studio,' I finished for him. Catriona's stupid Pilates. It had been bad enough when they were still together. Even after they'd split it was still making my life a misery. 'Dad, you have to ask for it back again.'

'That might be a bit . . .'

'And then you can pay Mum some rent, and everyone will be happy.'

'I'm not . . .'

I leaned my head on his shoulder, like I used to when I was tiny. 'And then everything will be OK and you can stay for as long as you want. You can do it, Dad!'

I couldn't see his face, but I felt his voice through his chest and down my ears and into my heart. 'For you, my princess, I'll give it a go.'

We sat, like that, for maybe a couple of minutes, the car going down the motorway so fast that it felt like we were flying – and I was perfectly, completely content.

CHAPTER SEVENTEEN

Everyone at the O2 seemed to know who I was without me having to tell them. I was swept through corridors, passed from one person to another like a human relay baton, from offices to dressing rooms, then around a corner and into a tunnel, until I was standing in the hot darkness behind a curtain along the edge of the stage, with little flutters of something in my stomach.

Nerves? Well, that made no sense, as there was nothing to be nervous about.

Probably just leftover angst from yesterday, I told myself, feeling the heat of the many, many, *many* people out in the crowd. I couldn't see them, but then, I didn't have to. I could hear them singing and chanting; feel their happiness, their excitement and their sheer energy. And as much as I wanted to find it pathetic, there was something a tiny bit infectious about all that joy. In fact—

'Katie, hi, hi.'

'Hi, Chris.' Beside me, Dad was looking expectant. 'Dad, this is Chris. He's a journalist. He's going to put me on the ten o'clock news.'

'Chris, hi – Benjamin Cox.' Dad gave him his best smile, the one that's like floodlights.

'Hello, Benjamin.'

There was an awful lot of helloing and shaking of hands. Then, finally, Chris said, 'So, we thought we'd interview you during "Clap Your Hands", the boys' new single, it's towards the end. If you just stay here and we'll set up, and then when the song begins, I'll start talking.'

'So I have to sit through a whole entire Karamel concert?' A guilty part of me thought how much Lacey would have loved it. In fact, I was wondering if I should ring her so she could listen in, and trying to work out whether I had enough minutes left to cover the whole thing when—

'You came!'

'Kurt. Hi. Um, yes, I came.'

He was standing RIGHT NEXT TO ME.

'I didn't think you would!'

'Well, I did,' I said. And Dad said:

'Benjamin Cox, musician. If you ever need someone...'

'Pleased to meet you, Mr Cox,' said Kurt, looking for all the world as though he was pleased to meet my dad.

He was dressed, completely stupidly, in this billowy shirt thing, over a pair of neat, sharp jeans. And his hair – it was sticking up in about thirty-seven thousand tufts, all pointing in different directions, like a kind of human mop.

'Have my card,' said Dad.

'Thanks,' said Kurt, sticking it into his back pocket. 'Hey, sorry, but I've got to go. The support finished ages ago, crowd's getting restless. See you after?'

'I don't know. It's a school night. I have homework.'

'What?' said Dad. '*Of course* we'll stick around.'

'Cool,' said Kurt. 'See you, then.'

I was just breathing a sigh of relief that he was off when he turned and shot me an awkward grin. 'Enjoy the show.'

'I really won't,' I said, to his departing back.

Now, the noise from the audience had gone from loud to supersonic, and around me, people with headsets and radios and things were running about, doing whatever it is that they do, which seemed mainly to be trying to change one of the light bulbs in a ten-foot-high letter 'K'.

'This is fab, isn't it?' said Dad. 'Ringside seats

 191

for your favourite band.'

'Where did you get that from?' I asked him. 'Karamel are not my favourite band. Not even close.'

'Really?' Dad sounded surprised.

'Did you, um, did you not, notice, that the new song, did you not notice what it was, you know, um, about?'

'The one about me? Which was brilliant, by the way. Might see if I can get Taylor to cover it.'

'No, the one about boy bands. Dad, you do know why we're here, don't you?'

Dad opened his mouth to reply. But then . . .

The lights blazed.

The crowd roared.

And Karamel bounded on to the stage like a basket of upturned puppies.

'HELLO THE O2! Are we feeling it?'

'No,' I murmured.

Kolin and Kristian were clapping, and – of course – it was absolutely right that Kurt managed a microphone *and* the lead guitar.

I sighed. 'That guitar is beautiful.'

'It's a Gibson Les Paul,' said Dad. 'Very nice.'

'Wasted on him.'

Dad said something, but I never heard what, because as he began to speak, they began to play, and a wall of sound crashed against the crowd, making them scream and flash and fling their hands into the air.

Like puppets, I thought, just as I noticed that my left foot was tapping to the beat.

'I said, ARE WE FEELING IT?'

Kurt's supple fingers were gliding across his guitar. Exactly the sort of fingers that those idiotic girls were probably imagining brushing across their backs, or running through their hair.

'Then let's go!'

Ugh, his confidence was revolting. He ought to have shown at least a bit of shame, if he had any self-respect whatsoever.

'We are so excited to be here tonight! We're gonna start with something new . . .'

Streaks of yellow fire shot up from the front of the stage as they began to sing and, there was no doubt about it, Kurt really could sing – and it was sort of uplifting:

WINGS BEAT FASTER IN MY HEART
KISS MY LIPS BEFORE WE PART

I found myself leaning in. Then leaning out, because, come on.

And then leaning back in again.

HURTS INSIDE BUT NOW I SEE
I MUST LET THE BIRD FLY FREE

I rubbed my finger across my wrist. Goosebumps.

LET THE BIRD FLY FREE

The darkness around me seemed to dissolve and now I was in a new place, where mayflies flitted above and droplets of dew shimmered in the summer light and . . . No, my ears were wrong, this was Karamel, it was hopeless and awful and . . .

LITTLE BIRD SO FREE

And then there was the way the chorus lifted and lingered, before collapsing into a glitter of notes that seemed to rain down over my head and . . .

FLY HOME BIRD
TO ME.

The final note held, then broke, and then, before I could even catch my breath:

'Now for our first ever number one. Get ready . . . for an All Night Part-aaaay!'

I tried to imagine I was somewhere else, listening to something halfway good, not this terrible rubbish that was making me sway and then pulling me on to my very tiptoes.

In fact, if I really concentrated, I could forget about Karamel altogether. Forget about the way that their music came at me like a sky full of doves, swooping and soaring, racing across fields, skimming the sea before hurtling up, up into the blue . . .

No, not birds, something rich and lovely, a chocolate cake with a million layers . . .

Forget the way Kurt's fingers slid across his guitar like it was a part of him, like he was running fast downhill with the wind behind him . . .

Oh my God.

'Sing with me, O2!'

 195

My hands were in the air and my vision began to cloud with bursts of gold. The lights, maybe, or perhaps it was the chords themselves, bursting out of the air, filling my eyes with the same fire that flowed from Kurt's fingers.

'Are you OK?' shouted Dad. 'Katie, you're shaking.'

'Help me,' I murmured, but my words were lost in the wonderful, awful, wonderful music.

CHAPTER EIGHTEEN

'Katie? Katie?'

Minutes, or maybe hours later, there was a tap on my shoulder.

'Katie, are you ready to go?'

'Whu . . . ?'

'Great!'

I just had time to realize that the person talking was Chris, that there was a TV camera pointing right into my face, when . . .

'So, Katie, tell me, what is it that you so dislike about Karamel?'

A few metres away, Kurt was bent over the microphone, eyes half closed.

'I, um, I don't like their music.'

'Yes, but why?'

'Because . . .' Wow, how had he just jumped an octave? *How?* 'It's very . . . I don't . . . it's not . . . very . . . good.'

'Twenty thousand people out there seem to disagree.'

'Yes. But. Yes.'

Chris gave me a funny look, then turned to talk into the lens. 'While Katie Cox never actually names the subject of her new single "Can't Stand the Boy Band", surely, Karamel, the world's number one boy band, must be who you're talking about?'

'Um, maybe.'

'You've been extremely vocal in your dislike of manufactured bands, of autotuning, even their expensive merchandise came in for criticism. As you said when we first spoke, who has forty pounds to spend on a T-shirt?'

'The T-shirts? Oh yeah. They're exploiting their fans,' I said, wondering vaguely whether Dad would lend me forty pounds.

'So to conclude, Katie, why should viewers buy your single and not theirs?'

Something about his rather narky tone pulled me out of my daze, and I managed to look into the camera and say, 'Because they are fake, and I am the real deal. I'm Katie Cox and my music is true. That's why.'

'With the two singles now out and battling for the top spot in the charts, only time will tell. Handing back to the studio now for the news.'

▶

The maddest thing is that I can't even remember the end of their set. I must have been ill or something. Certainly my head was sort of burning, although in another way I think I experienced every single moment more vividly than anything that had ever happened to me before.

The last notes died away and the three of them ran from the stage.

Dad was looking around. 'Come on. Let's go find this party, shall we?'

'I don't know,' I said. And I didn't. I didn't know anything about anything.

'You need something to eat,' said Dad. 'They always have food at these things.'

He guided me down some steps, me stumbling like I'd only just got over the flu, and then went off through an open door, and I could hear music and laughter, and I stood, my head resting on the wall, my eyes half closed, trying to make some kind of sense of what was happening to me . . .

'Well? Still think we're plastic?'

I opened my eyes, and there he was.

'Yes, actually,' I said. 'You totally had a wind machine. That bit where you all walked forward, with your shirts

 199

flapping about? That is *exactly* what I was talking about.'

'Ha! Yeah, all right. But—'

'And you all sat on bar stools. Er, cliché much?'

'They were not bar stools! They were . . . just . . . high stools that we . . . all right, they were bar stools.'

'And that video, the one they projected while you did the song about the party. With you all jumping around. You were on a camper van. And then you all walked off into the sea at the end!'

He was really laughing now. 'You know why we had our backs to the camera? It was so cold when we were filming that Kristian was crying.'

'Really? Ha!'

'Anyway. Thanks for coming. I'm sorry you didn't like it. I've never played like that before. I wanted you to . . . I'm just sorry that I couldn't convince you that we're not what you think we are.'

I could sort of feel my heart hammering in my chest, the blood pulsing in the very tips of my fingers, as I said:

'There were a few bits that I didn't completely hate.'

He looked up. 'Wow. The praise is too much for me to bear.'

'I liked that riff you did on the beginning of the one about your mum.'

'Huh. I was trying to be The Edge.'

'Well, you weren't. But, it still sounded good. And that first song, the bird one, was . . . kind of . . . amazing.' There was a silence. My breathing felt far too loud. To cover it up, I said, 'Plus, you have an OK voice.'

'Just OK?' He laughed that lovely laugh. 'Katie, fess up. I saw you cheering.'

'I was not.'

'You started out just standing there. By "Big Love" you were jumping up and down. And at the end there I could see you singing along.'

'Stalker!' I had to stop myself from thrilling at the idea that even while he had all of the O2 to sing to, he'd noticed me.

'Should've got you onstage.'

'In front of that many people? I don't understand how you can do it.'

'I wasn't confident to begin with,' said Kurt, like he was telling me this great secret. Maybe he was. He was talking fast, his cheeks all flushed. 'But . . . I love being onstage, making music. It's the only time I ever feel

 201

like I'm really being me.'

'I feel that too,' I mumbled. 'Like, I can't say stuff well at all, I'm totally failing English, half the time I can't even have a proper conversation. Lacey, she's my best mate, she's always getting the wrong end of the stick, she reckons I have verbal dyslexia, which I don't think is a thing but if it is I absolutely have it. Only, when I'm singing . . .'

'You're being your true self,' said Kurt.

'Yes.'

I had to make a conscious effort to remember that I didn't like him.

'It's funny,' Kurt was saying. 'I saw your video of "Just Me", and it was like, like a bomb going off in my head. I thought – I understand her. I get where she's coming from. That sound, pure, spontaneous – we need to get back to that.'

'Really?'

'Yeah,' said Kurt. 'And then, when I heard "Can't Stand the Boy Band" . . . it hurt.'

My phone was going in my pocket. Mum. Many, many missed calls. 'Look, I have to get home. Where's Dad?'

We looked across the room to see him laughing in the

middle of a big group of people.

'Your dad's pretty fun. I loved that song you did about him.'

'Thanks,' I said. 'Everyone else hated it.'

'It's nice that you're close. Mine went off when I was seven. Came back when the band got big, of course.' He dropped his eyes. 'Anyway. Doesn't matter.'

'I'm lucky,' I said.

'You are.'

There was this moment.

'About this stupid chart battle . . .' he began.

'Oh. That.'

'May the best man—'

'Or woman,' I said quickly.

'May the best man or woman win.'

Then he turned, and went into his party.

CHAPTER NINETEEN

'So to conclude, Katie, why should viewers buy your single and not theirs?'

'Because they are fake, and I am the real deal. I'm Katie Cox and my music is true. That's why.'

'With the two singles now out and battling for the top spot in the charts, only time will tell.'

I looked up from Paige's iPad and across our form room to see Savannah's top lip curl in a way that, on anyone else, would not have been pretty. Since it was on Savannah, it was still quite pretty.

'Babes, what happened?'

'Were you nervous?' said Paige.

'Um, I suppose so.'

'Because that was –' Savannah searched for a word, then, not finding one, went with two – 'car-crashy.'

'It wasn't that bad,' said Lacey.

'My boyfriend Kolin is seriously upset about it all,' said Savannah. 'I mean, he's totally rising above it because that's what he's like, but he is upset.'

'I'm sorry I upset Kolin,' I murmured.

'I think Kolin can look after himself,' said Lacey.

'But you were so weird,' said Sofie. 'It's like you'd forgotten how to speak, or something.'

'Like she was ill. Or mad. Like she was having a breakdown!'

And I was starting to think that maybe I was, when Lacey spoke up.

'Come on, Katie, let's go.'

We went down the main stairs, past the drama noticeboard, which was crowded with drama types all looking at some drama thing, and then the sports noticeboard, crowded by sports types all looking at some sports thing.

'Sorry about Savannah,' said Lacey.

'Hey, that's OK,' I said. 'It's not like you're in charge of her.'

Lacey scrunched up her face. A face that, I noticed, was lightly coated in some kind of moisturizer that made her look sort of damp.

'What?' said Lacey, her hand going to her cheek.

'Just, your skin . . . ?'

'Oh. Yeah. It's supposed to be "dewy".'

'You want your face to look like wet grass?'

'I did when Sofie got us all sample bottles. Is it awful?'

'No. Just a bit shiny.'

She smushed it around with her palms, leaving two patches of pink. 'Better?'

'A bit. But, Lace, don't let me stop you from looking dewy.'

'I won't,' said Lacey, slowing down to give the vending machine a longing stare. 'I'm stopping myself. Anyway, if I wanted to buy a pot, it'd be thirty-eight quid. So it was never going to be a long-term thing.'

I wanted to ask her whether she actually liked hanging out with Savannah and co., but maybe that was my answer. Reaching into my pocket, I found a pound coin, and popped it in. 'Whaddya want?'

'Oooh. Kit Kat?'

There's always a worry with vending machines that the chocolate will get stuck and then I'll shake the thing to try to get it out and the whole lot will tip over and crush me to death, which apparently happens more often than you'd think. I once said this to Amanda, who replied that I worry too much, and told me that people get killed

206

by everything, from bee stings to their own bed linen, which gave me even more to fret about. Luckily, on this occasion at least, the Kit Kat came tumbling straight down into the bottom.

'Here.' I offered Lacey half, and she took it. 'Um, you know . . . in the interview . . . on the TV last night . . . Was I really that bad?'

'You were fan-freaking-tastic,' said Lacey.

Which meant that yes, I was.

'I wish you'd been at the concert with me,' I said, and I did wish it, too. 'You keep me sane.'

'I wish I'd been there. You watched Karamel from the side of the stage. What a waste.'

'Lacey,' I began, 'what I told you. About . . . them. Karamel. I think maybe I said some stuff I didn't mean. Well, that I did mean, at the time, but now . . .'

Lacey was now into her second stick of Kit Kat, peeling away the last few flecks of silver foil. 'Katie, it's OK. I understand.'

'You do? Thank goodness! So here's the thing, I'd heard them before, of course I had. But I'd never *heard* them, until last night. And—'

'And now you're lying about how you feel to be my

friend again.' I was about to set her straight, when she carried on. 'Which is really nice of you and everything. But, I don't want you to tell me that you like them.'

'You don't?'

'You're you, Katie, and you hate Karamel. You don't like their music or their fashion or their high production values or even that they're popular. You hate the mainstream. And that's not something we agree on, honestly, but it's who you are and you are my friend and your life is difficult enough right now without me abandoning you too.'

'Um.'

'Friends forever!' said Lacey.

'Er, yes.'

'It's like you said. You're real and you're true. And sometimes we're going to disagree. But you need to be able to be yourself. Or what's the point of us being mates?'

'Mmm.'

She took a bite, then grinned at me, a tiny blob of chocolate on her front tooth. 'So, what was the worst thing about last night? The most annoying thing they did? You're going to tell me anyway, so I might as well ask and get it out the way.'

I was feeling extremely uncomfortable, and not only because Amanda had shrunk my skirt in the wash.

'I don't know that I could pick a specific moment. There was a chord sequence that went into this song about a sunset beach, it was actually technically incredibly accomplished . . . and also very, very bad. In a technically accomplished way.'

Lacey threw a handful of wrapper at the bin. 'What else? Go on, you know you want to.'

'Er. OK. I didn't like the way Kurt – that's his name, right? – Kurt looked out into the audience like he was about to kiss them all. He did this thing with his eyes. And his hands. It made me feel weird.' That, at least, was true.

'I know what you mean,' said Lacey. 'It does seem a bit like they want all their fans to be in love with them so they can sell them music. And, I dunno. I've been thinking. And I do love them. But—'

'Because I've been thinking too,' I said, quickly, 'and I don't mind if you want to talk about them a bit. Like, not loads, because you're right, it's way boring. But if you, say, wanted to lend me a couple of their albums or something then we could play them and chat about them, maybe after school tomorrow if you want? Bring everything you have.'

'I don't want to do that,' said Lacey. 'Because I know you wouldn't like it.'

'I'm just saying, if you *did*, then I'd be totally up for it. As a favour to you. Tomorrow. Or tonight. Or the day after tomorrow, if you'd rather. Whenever, basically.'

'Katie, it's fine.'

'No,' I said. 'It's not. I know you're pretending you don't care about them as much as you did, but secretly deep down I think that you do. And so I am willing to put my . . . er . . . prejudices aside, for one night only, or a few nights, and do a complete Karamelathon, completely immerse myself in their work, in order to save our friendship.'

'That's very generous of you, Katie. But honestly, our friendship doesn't need saving.'

'Doesn't it? Because, I dunno, recently, I've been getting the feeling that –'

I stopped, because Lacey wasn't looking at me. She was looking at her phone.

And I did think, if this girl is about to tell me we are BFFs while simultaneously texting Savannah, then I will . . .

'Look, K.'

She held it out. There, in her iTunes library, was 'Can't Stand the Boy Band'. Artist, Katie Cox.

'I bought it.'

'But you already have it. I sent it to you. Way back. That's how all this started.'

'Yeah, but Katie, this is a chart battle. And if there's going to be a battle, of course I'm fighting for you.'

'Oh, Lace.'

Sensing that I was about to do something incredibly embarrassing like cry in the corridor, she brought out a pair of headphones. 'Shall we?'

We looped them in one ear each, and sat on the dining hall steps, very close.

 Can't stand the boy band

'It's you!' Lacey squeezed my hand. 'Your new single.'

'Yes.'

'You were so worried, and now, here it is. I'm proud of you, GF.'

'Thank you,' I said, in my smallest voice. We listened, as well as we could over the noise of a load of year sevens coming past. Even with that, and with the fact that I could only hear it through my right ear, I caught a scratch in my voice as I went into

⏸ On the skin that's perma-tanned

Plus, the guitar seemed thin, all on its own, without even a bass line to shore it up. My brain reminded me of the lushness that was Karamel, and I found myself saying:

'You don't think it sounds a bit, er, underproduced?'

'To me it does,' said Lacey. 'But then, we know I like my music overproduced. So I don't think my opinion counts.'

'It does!' For the second time in ten minutes I found myself wanting to cry. 'Your opinion totally counts!'

'It doesn't,' insisted Lacey, 'because I don't know about music like you do.'

'Maybe I don't know about music. Maybe I've been shouting my mouth off about something without taking the trouble to really understand it.'

She smiled. 'You wouldn't do that.'

'Lacey,' I said, because I was genuinely worried that my head might explode or fall off or something, 'I've got to go.'

'Now?'

'Yes.'

'But . . . we're listening.'

'I know.' I had to get away. 'Sorry. But I have a bus to catch.'

'Can't you get the next one?'

'No. I said I'd be home for six. It's the chart announcement.'

'Good luck,' said Lacey. 'Not that you need it.'

Death by Vending Machine

You can die by duvet
Or pillowcase
You can die from a storm
If you're in the wrong place
You can die from bouncing off a trampoline
Or being crushed by a chocolate vending machine

You can die by wasp
You can die by bee
You can die from slipping
On a single pea
Or getting caught in the wheels of a pink limousine
Or being crushed by a chocolate vending machine

You can die onstage
Or in your room
You can die of guilt
You can die of gloom
You can die of regret for what might have been
Or being crushed by a chocolate vending machine.

CHAPTER TWENTY

Twenty minutes later I was curled up on the front seat of the bus with my head resting on the window, its frame vibrating against my cheek. I had my lyric book out, but for some reason the page kept filling up with curly *K*'s, plus the occasional *aramel*. All right, more than occasional.

'What are you writing?'

Jaz had strayed from her usual backseat territory to come and peer over my shoulder.

'Just songs,' I said, moving my palm to cover the page. Which, to any normal person, would have been a signal that my words were private and not to be looked at.

Unfortunately, while Jaz had clearly noticed part one of the signal, part two was not on the agenda. She shoved my hand out of the way and stared.

'Why do you keep writing the word "Karamel"?'

'That doesn't say Karamel,' I said.

We both looked at the tangle of biro. It very obviously did say Karamel.

'Because I hate them so much.'

Jaz didn't seem ever so satisfied with this explanation. 'Are you secretly obsessing about Karamel?'

'Lay off, Jaz. I'm not secretly anything.'

'Touchy.'

'I am *not* being touchy!' It came out disturbingly high, like I'd sucked in helium. Which Amanda had done once, at Cousin Dean's wedding, and then freaked out about it and had a very squeaky panic attack. 'I'm so not!'

Clearly sensing she was on to something, Jaz leaned in.

'Ve-ery touchy.'

Time to do some damage control. I straightened my features and pushed back my hair and cleared my throat. 'Jaz. Listen. I know you like a bit of scandal and I get that you think you're on to something here. But, if you remember, I hate Karamel. Really hate them. I hate them so much that I've written a song about exactly how much I hate them, which is loads.'

'Fair enough,' said Jaz.

'Good. I'm glad we've got that sorted.'

The bus rumbled along for a bit and I allowed myself to relax. The car behind us honked. And I was just feeling my cheeks get back to a normal kind of temperature when:

'I'm just saying,' said Jaz. 'If there's anything you want to get off your chest . . .'

'There isn't!' I said.

'Because if there is . . . ?'

'There is not.'

'Are you sure?' said Jaz.

'I am sure.'

'Really sure?'

And then, I knew it was crazy and I knew I shouldn't, but I had to tell someone . . . because it was too difficult to keep it all secret, like I was a glass, and someone was pouring water into me, more and more and more until I was overflowing. Jaz had probably figured it out by now anyway with her weirdo psychic Jaz skills. Plus, saying it out loud just felt right.

'. . . and they began to play and I realized I'd heard them loads of times, but I'd never really *heard* them. And then I did and it was amazing! Like nothing I've ever felt before, Jaz. It was mind-blowing. My mind was blown. Is blown! It was like . . . like religion, or something! They are so incredibly talented! Like, a zillion times more than anyone else in the world who's ever lived! The stuff they can do . . . The sound they make . . . And Kurt, he's kind and he's funny and he's so, so sweet. You know, he didn't have to forgive me for hating on him, it really upset him, but he did because he's ace. And as far as the rest of the world is concerned I can't stand Karamel, when in fact I can't seem to stop obsessing about them. Oh, Jaz, what am I going to do?'

'Yeah, I was not expecting that,' said Jaz.

When I got home, Dad was in the kitchen, riffling through a heap of takeaway menus.

'Katie, what would you like for dinner tonight?'

'Er. It's just, we're kind of waiting for the big announcement. About the whole chart thing. So I'm a bit . . .'

'Food's on me! Anything you fancy?'

I was feeling more sick than hungry, so I just said, 'Chinese please. Proper takeaway, not an Asda box.'

'Done! Where's your mother?'

'Here,' said Mum, taking off her jacket. 'I've just had a text from Ade, he's stuck in traffic, he'll be back in a mo, and . . . will you please get off me, Benjamin.'

'Zoe, don't say I never spend money on you!' He had his hand on her waist. 'What would you like, my princess? Anything at all.'

Mum's eyes said she'd like for Dad to go away, but she said:

'Chinese takeaway is fine.'

'Chinese takeaway it is!' He spun her in a little circle. Or at least, he tried to. Mum wasn't really having it, so he got her halfway round and then bashed her into the oven. 'Sorry, Zo.'

A big sigh.

'And look,' he said. 'This is . . . important. It's meant a lot, you giving me a place to stay. Really, it has.'

Mum mumbled something that might have been, 'S'OK.'

'And I know we're family and you'd always do it for me . . .'

Another sigh.

'But still. I appreciate it, my darling. Now, will you take this and go buy yourself something nice?'

And – whoah – he handed her this MASSIVE lump of cash.

Mum was as shocked as I was. So shocked, in fact, that

at first she didn't say anything, but just made fish faces. Then, finally, 'Benj. This is . . . too much.'

He dipped his head. 'I owe you.'

'Well, yes, you probably do, in fact, you definitely do, but this, this is –' she thumbed through it – 'thousands.'

'A couple of thousand. Don't spend it all at once! Or, do! Take yourself into town, dress up nice for a change. Talking of which . . .' He leaned down behind the table, and lifted up this vast cardboard box. 'Here, Katie. For you.'

'Right.' Then, as I clocked what was written on the box – which was the word 'Gibson': 'Seriously? Like, *seriously*?'

'Open it!' said Dad, with that expression I recognized from Christmas Day.

I tore into the box. And there, nestled down among a load of bits of polystyrene . . . was quite literally the most beautiful guitar I'd ever seen.

'Oh my God, Dad. Oh my God.'

'You like?'

I threw my arms around him.

'I love it. And I love you.'

'I got something for your sister too.' He hesitated, then took a little box out of his pocket. A little box in Tiffany blue. Blimey. He really had gone shopping. 'Do you think you could give it to her for me?'

'Of course,' I said, and then, when Mum pushed off to the loo, I caught his arm. 'Hey, I'm so glad you talked to Catriona.'

'I . . . uh . . . no problem. Anything for my little superstar.'

'I'm not a superstar yet.'

'You're going to be number one,' said Dad. 'I just know it.'

'I'd be happy with top twenty,' I said.

'Number one,' said Dad. 'Come on, Katie. Dare to dream! And, let's get this Chinese ordered, shall we? Always takes longer than they say, and I'm starving.'

I'd just opened the menu and was trying to decide whether Dad's newfound generosity would stretch to beef in black-bean sauce *and* chicken-and-prawn chow mein, when the front door slammed in that heavy way that meant it was—

'Ade,' said Mum.

'Haveyouheardanynewspleasetellme,' I said.

'Let the man take off his jacket,' said Mum.

Which I did, and it took about a hundred years.

'They beat me, didn't they? Tell me that it was close, at least.'

'Chillax,' said Adrian, despite some very specific instructions from me never to use that word. 'It's not out yet. Tony's going to text me. But, look, whatever happens now, I want you to know how proud I am. How proud we all are.'

'Yes, yes,' I said. Then, because that sounded a bit ungrateful, 'And thank you. For supporting me. I know I've made things difficult recently. And, you know, not recently. But anyway. Thank you.'

'You've been standing up for what you believe,' said Adrian. 'Of course it's difficult. But it's worth doing.' He glanced at the clock. 'Any minute now.'

Mum took my hand.

Dad took my other hand.

Ding!

Adrian picked up the phone, his forehead creasing.

'Well? WELL? Tell me! Actually, don't tell me. I can't bear it. No, do tell me. Tell me!'

'Katie,' said Adrian. 'Karamel's single debuted at number two.'

'*AND?*'

'And yours is at number seventy-eight.'

CHAPTER TWENTY-ONE

'It's fine,' I said. 'It's exactly what I was expecting. It's completely fine.'

Three concerned faces stared across the table at me, like a load of sad owls.

'I mean, come on!' I told them. 'They're a massively successful boy band with squillions of fans. I'm just me. There was no way I was ever going to even come close to winning this.'

Mum went to squeeze my shoulder, and then saw my face and thought better of it.

'You don't need to feel sorry for me.'

'Love,' said Mum. 'This industry, I don't want to see you hurt . . .'

'I'm not hurt,' I said. 'I am annoyed. But I always knew this would happen. Can we please not talk about it any more.'

'Well . . .' Mum began.

'I mean it,' I said. After all, how could she even begin to understand? She didn't get it, she couldn't get it. Not

  223

her, and not Adrian. In fact, there was only one person who could.

'Dad. I –'

He looked away. 'I'll go pick up that Chinese, shall I? Won't be a tick, it's, what, ten minutes' walk? Not paying the delivery charge if I don't have to.'

'OK. But maybe don't get anything for me. Turns out I'm not hungry!'

I walked, very slowly, up to my room.

Then I sat down at my desk and burst into tears.

There's a reason that people in films generally cry while face down on a bed, or sliding off the back of a door.

You don't see them crying on to a desk, and that's because, as I quickly discovered, crying directly on to a desk is incredibly uncomfortable. Plus, when I finally sat up, I found that I'd been leaning on a red felt-tip pen and it looked like my cheek had been burned.

The best music had won.

I'd known it when Lace and I had listened to my song, on the dining room steps. Heck, I'd known it the second Kurt had opened his mouth at the Karamel concert.

What should I do now?

What *could* I do now?

I could tell the world that I'd changed my mind. No, not changed my mind, more that when I'd written 'Can't Stand the Boy Band' I hadn't known what I was talking about.

That was Old Katie. New Katie had seen Karamel play. She was converted. New Katie loved Karamel.

Then, I'd shake their hands, if they'd let me, and . . .

Ding!

Just heard. Coming over

Lacey. My best, best, best friend. She'd stick with me. She'd understand that everyone makes mistakes.

Ding!

Just heard am coming over

So loyal that she'd sent the same text twice!

Plus, it would be good to come clean with Lace. Once she'd forgiven me, it would make our friendship even stronger.

That's the thing about me and Lace. We've had our

ups and downs, for sure, and the downs have been quite bad. But it's what makes the rest of the time together so great. Like, for example, when we had that monster argument over who copied whose *Julius Caesar* essay. Now we're over it, we're better mates than ever. Even though, come to think of it, she never did admit that she'd nabbed her introduction from me, and to be honest it's still a tiny bit annoying.

BANG BANG BANG!

Lacey was thumping on the front door. I scampered down the stairs and opened it, arms wide for a full-on hug, and:

'Hi,' said Jaz.

'What? What are you doing here?'

'I texted,' said Jaz.

'No,' I told her. '*Lacey* texted. Lacey is on her way over.'

'Hi,' said Lacey, coming up the drive. 'What? Why so surprised? Did you not get my message? And what's *she* doing here?'

'Supporting Katie,' said Jaz.

'*I'm* supporting Katie,' said Lacey. 'Urgh! What happened to your cheek? Is that a burn?!'

Unscheduled gatherings are normally a complete no-no. I thought Mum would probably cut me some slack, given current events, but I still made sure to get everyone upstairs and into my bedroom as speedily as possible.

'It's just disgusting,' said Lacey, as I closed the door behind her. 'They can't be content with winning. They have to crush you. How dare they? How actually dare they?'

'It's not their fault,' I said. 'They have a massive fan base and they're really g– . . . some people think they are really good.'

'You should have won,' said Lacey.

'Nah,' I said.

'You're so real and true and they're just this manufactured . . .'

'It is a bit unfair,' I said. 'I mean, talk about David and Goliath.'

'Are David and Goliath in Karamel?' said Jaz. 'I thought they all began with a K.'

'You know nothing,' said Lacey.

Jaz didn't flinch. 'I know more than you think,' she said.

Lacey gave her a superior smile. 'Hey, look, Jaz, it's great that you're here, but me and Katie, we're best

 227

mates and we have some stuff we need to talk about.'

Jaz picked up my liquid eyeliner and gazed down at the bottle. 'Oh, so now you're here for her, are you?'

'Yes. I am.'

'Now that you can pity her?'

This is why it's important to keep friends as separate as possible. Ideally on different continents. Mind you, the way Lacey was looking at Jaz at that moment, even continents wouldn't have been enough to stop World War III starting. Different planets?

'You are poison, you know that, Jaz?'

'Lacey . . .' I began.

'Fine,' said Lacey. 'But she is.'

I have to say that Jaz wasn't at all bothered by Lacey's accusations. She just sat there, using my liquid eyeliner to give my Amy Winehouse poster a moustache.

'They just made an announcement,' said Lacey, reading from her phone. "*Peace and love to all our fans who bought the single, and to all who bought Katie Cox's song. The music lives forever. Xo*". That is rude!'

'Um, yeah. So rude.'

Lacey lay back on my bed and twiddled her hair. 'You

228

know what? I think I'm starting to get why you're so annoyed by them.'

This was it. The moment to come clean. 'Lacey?'

'Yes?'

I must have said it in a fairly significant-sounding way because she sat up and let her hair drop.

The words were all ready, lined up in neat rows inside my mouth, like a little wordy army, poised to fight for the truth.

And they did come out. But not from me.

'Katie has something to tell you,' said Jaz.

'What?' I said.

'What?' said Lacey.

'I'm surprised she hasn't said it already. Given that you're "best mates".'

'I'm sure she did tell me,' said Lacey. 'Katie tells me everything.'

'Did she tell you that she's in love with Karamel?' said Jaz.

'WHAT?' said Lacey.

Which is when I knew I couldn't say it.

Not here.

Not now.

 229

'Of course I'm not in love with Karamel. Jaz, you are being mad. Where would you even get that from?'

Jaz's face hardened. And it was pretty hard already. 'Cool. I'll just let you get on with it, then.'

'Get on with what?'

'Living your lie.'

'I'm not living a lie.'

'Go away, Jaz,' said Lacey. 'Get back to wherever it is you came from and leave me and my BFF alone.'

Jaz's head swivelled from me to Lacey and back again and she blinked a couple of times, but she didn't seem even slightly fazed. That's the thing about Jaz. You can't hurt her. She's made of whatever they use to line saucepans.

'I'm leaving,' she said.

'Good,' said Lacey.

'No, stay,' I said, weakly. 'Unless it's important. Or, you know, not important.'

And then she'd gone.

'Where does she get that rubbish?' said Lacey.

'I know,' I said, hating myself, and Jaz, and myself all over again.

'So?' said Lacey. 'What are you going to say to them? You can't let this stand.'

I opened my laptop, and thought for a second. Lacey was watching the screen as I typed:

To all the fans who bought my single, THANK YOU. Karamel – u guys still suck. And yr army of zombies doesn't change anything. Rock & roll K x

I hit return. 'Right. Done. It's all finished.'

'Finished?' said Lacey, the colour rising in her cheeks, like when Mum has that cocktail involving cranberry and orange juice. 'This is just the beginning.'

'Of what?' I said.

'Your comeback.'

'Oh. Because I was kind of thinking I might shut up for a bit.'

The flush was now all the way to the top of Lacey's face. 'It's not like *nobody* bought the single. You're at seventy-eight!'

'Which is rubbish.'

'It is not rubbish. It's really good and you are only going to get better. You are going to build on your fan base and you are going to write more great songs. I believe in you, Katie.'

'That's great, Lace,' I said. 'But, honestly, I'm not sure that I do.'

There was a weird sound, like a cat mewing, and for a second I thought maybe the mice had learned a new skill, only then I realized it was Lacey's phone.

'New ringtone,' said Lacey, bouncing to her feet. 'Sofie did it for me. Do you want it for yours?'

I shook my head.

'Mum's outside in the car,' said Lacey. 'Gotta go, K.'

'Thanks for coming.'

'I'm so glad I did,' said Lacey. 'Remember: you are—'

'Don't say it!'

'And you'll always be—'

'Please . . .'

'*My* number one,' said Lacey.

'Ugh, you are so cheesy,' I said. 'Get out.'

She got out.

I was on my own.

The bedroom felt incredibly empty. Like there were too many spaces between the molecules of air. Spaces that, under any normal circumstance, I would have filled with music.

Something like . . . I scrolled through my playlists . . .

Amy? Nah, too dark. Mraz? Too light.

What I needed was . . .

No.

No . . .

Yes.

A quick few taps and there they were, three boys beaming from my screen, the notes flowing through my headphones and lifting me up and away from all the weirdness, on to a golden cloud where everything was still OK.

Lacey was completely right. It had all been a bit humiliating, but I'd come through just fine. Number seventy-eight wasn't nothing. People still basically liked me. Lacey still liked me.

Thank goodness I hadn't told her the truth.

CHAPTER TWENTY-TWO

Jaz wasn't on the bus come Monday morning. I'd got so used to her presence on the back seat that to see it empty was a bit of a shock. A couple of the year sevens had a quick go at plunking their bums into her place, then bounced back up again, as though she was somehow watching and might swoop in and destroy them.

She really wasn't there, though. I had to remind myself that, historically, Jaz had always had a pretty relaxed attitude to things like attendance and learning. Her absence didn't necessarily mean anything.

I suppose I was particularly sensitive to things because everyone was being a bit odd. Towards me.

It started with a year seven girl bashing me with her bag as we got on to the bus, in a way that could have been an accident but clearly wasn't. After that, no one said anything to me at all. Fin didn't even bother trying to shake his finished crisp packet over my head. I suppose I should have been grateful.

Only, coming off my weird weekend, I suppose I was just feeling a bit uneasy. Mum and Adrian were being so relentlessly positive that I could barely look at them. Dad, meanwhile, jumped out of his seat every time I came into the room, like he was waiting for me to combust or melt down, and Amanda, well, I'd barely seen her. I was quite looking forward to getting to school, which is saying something.

As I walked through the door of the form room, I heard someone say:

'Here she is.'

And someone else say:

'This is going to be interesting.'

And then Paige and Sofie just came at me like they were a pair of pigeons and I was a chip:

'Katie, it's . . . ?'

'What are you . . . ?'

Then they ran out of words.

'Can someone please tell me what has happened?'

Silence. The whole form just stared.

'Someone? *Anyone?*'

The crowd parted to reveal Savannah, her beautiful face looking beautifully pale.

'We've seen. Don't try to deny it, Katie. We all know.'

Holding out her gold-plated phone like it was some kind of religious offering, she began to walk towards me in these slow steps that seemed designed to make me want to scream. Luckily, I didn't have to wait the five minutes it would have taken for her to get to me; I just leaned forward and snatched it.

HYPOCRITE

In her latest single, teen sensation Katie Cox tells us that she hates boy bands. But we know better.

An unnamed source, speaking exclusively to Pop Trash, told how Cox, watching from the wings of the Karamel concert, laughed, smiled, clapped and sang to lead singer Kurt Thorpe, before engaging in a long and personal chat just after the show ended. Whatever she's been telling her fans, Ms Cox clearly has ideas of her own.

The revelations come after what was billed by Top Music as the greatest chart battle in twenty years, between Cox's brand of 'real' music and the more processed sound so beloved of Karamel's fans. Thorpe took to social media to state, 'Peace and love to all our fans who bought the single, and to all who bought Katie Cox's song,' while Cox's account carried the message, 'Karamel – u guys still suck'.

Despite her strong words, in her interview with NTV news, Cox appeared unsettled. Clearly coming so close to her idols left the young singer-songwriter a little hot under the collar.

With her single languishing at the bottom of the charts, we ask, is now the time for Katie Cox to come clean about her deception? Her remaining fans surely deserve the truth.

'Yeah.' I looked up from the phone to see Lacey, right in front of me. She was gripping Savannah's hand. 'I think a bit of truth would be nice.'

'But . . . where . . . how did they . . . who . . . ?'

'That's today's Pop Trash,' said Paige, who I think thought she was being helpful. 'And it's on TMZ too, and

MailOnline and Jezebel and Just Jared. And E! And Perez Hilton did this whole thing . . . I'll send it to you if you want.'

'It's not true,' I said, hopelessly. It was, after all, absolutely true.

'You lie and you lie and you lie,' said Lacey.

'I . . .'

'It explains so much!' She was talking more to herself than she was to me. 'Why you were humming "Clap Your Hands" in the loo last week. Why you didn't invite me to their concert with you. Why you wanted me to come over and play all their songs.'

I couldn't speak.

'And you told *Jaz*?'

I still couldn't speak. Instead, I found myself looking down at my wrist and fiddling like crazy with my birthday charm bracelet, as if there was a chance that some tiny chunks of silver might save me, which there was no way they could.

'I don't want you wearing that,' said Lacey. 'Take it off.'

Everything seemed to go dark.

'It's very hard,' said another voice. 'I mean, obvs, I've known Katie for a while and we're in the same form. But

I think my loyalties have to be with my boyfriend Kolin, because he is very upset and completely blameless and he is my boyfriend so I do need to be there for him right now, since he is my boyfriend. Also, Katie is clearly rotten to the core.'

'You're a very loyal person, Savannah.'

'I know. I can't help it.'

A buzz of conversation around me, and then Ms McAllister's voice,

'Good morning, everyone. Savannah, that skirt is not even close to regulation length. I would ask you take it off, but I doubt I'd notice. Please go to the office right now and ask for something from lost property. And someone catch Katie, she is clearly about to faint.'

Then I was on the floor, my form teacher's face filling my vision. 'Katie?'

'I'm all right,' I said.

'You are grey,' said McAllister. 'Lacey, take Katie to the sick room.'

'No,' said Lacey.

'Wh— oh, for goodness sake. I will take her myself.' Then, like she was Tarzan and I was Jane, McAllister lifted me into her arms. 'The rest of you, assembly.'

It was Dad who drove me home, in a smart silver car I'd not seen before.

'A Honda Jazz, would you believe? And I asked for a brand-new BMW!'

'What? Where?' I was still having trouble forming sentences.

'Car rental. Your Adrian didn't seem to want me to borrow his any more, so I made the trip to Hertz.' He thumped the wheel. 'The joys of the open road!'

'Umph.'

'You all right?'

'Er, not really. That's why I've been sent home from school.'

'I thought you were just faking!'

'No,' I said. 'I feel terrible.'

'Don't puke on the upholstery, will you?'

'I won't.'

I managed to stagger up the drive and into my bedroom, Dad standing in the doorway.

'Can I get you anything, princess?'

I managed a laugh. 'Did you see the stories?' After four tries, I managed to unhook the bracelet, and I dropped it on to my bedside table, where it sat in a sad little heap. 'Maybe you could get me a new life.'

He flapped a hand. 'That rubbish? Ignore it!'

'Dad . . . I can't.'

'By this time tomorrow everyone will have forgotten it.' He patted his pocket. 'Got to go, K. You have a little sleep. Your mum'll be up soon.'

I did try to sleep, but it's not easy at eleven in the morning, even for someone as good at it as me.

All I could think was that someone had betrayed me.

Jaz?

Jaz.

No wonder she hadn't come to school.

Only . . .

No, of course it was her.

Of course it was.

> Can't believe u went to Pop Trash, Jaz.
>
> I thought we were friends

The message came back a moment later.

Can't believe you think I'd do that.
And I thought we were friends 2.

But . . .

U were the only one I told

Katie, read the article properly. I wasn't at the concert was I

I read it again. And – aargh – she was right.

> An unnamed source, speaking exclusively to Pop Trash, told how Cox, watching from the wings of the Karamel concert laughed, smiled, clapped and sang to lead singer Kurt Thorpe, before engaging in a long and personal chat just after the show ended.

Jaz couldn't have known that.

Soz Jaz

No reply.

So if it wasn't Jaz, then it had to be someone else.

 242

Of course. It was so obvious. I don't know why I'd ever thought it was Jaz.

When it was Kurt.

He had seen me cheer for him. He knew I was still releasing my song.

I'd betray me, under the same circumstances.

Only . . . when we'd talked, I suppose I'd thought we had some kind of connection, in a way I'd never really had with a boy before. Scratch that, in a way I'd never really had with anyone.

Which just made me hate him more.

I opened my laptop.

KTCoX: Shocked Kurt_Karamel would sell me out like that just 2 get his single to chart

In my head I could hear Amanda and Lacey telling me that I should step away from the keyboard. But only in my head. It wasn't like either of them was actually there.

I hit return.

Kurt_Karamel: Nothing to do with me. But v glad to hear u r a fan ☺

KTCoX: U sold me 2 the press

Kurt_Karamel: I would never do that. You know I wouldn't.

Which did sort of feel true.

Then I caught myself. Never mind feelings. The point was, he had.

KTCoX: I know what I see

Kurt_Karamel: Out of line, Katie. You need to apologize right now

KTCoX: U need to apologize. To me and to all of HUMANITY

Which felt pretty satisfying, I can tell you.

What could he possibly come back with?

I waited.

And waited.

Then I refreshed.

And refreshed, and refreshed.

 244

And, nothing. Except that, after a few seconds, his feed vanished.

He'd only gone and BLOCKED me!

Which kind of said it all.

And I'd *trusted* him.

I let out a howl.

'What? Are you all right? Your father said you'd come home from school . . .'

Mum's head came poking round the door. She looked exhausted. Night shifts always take it out of her, but this was something worse.

'I came over a bit funny,' I said, as she padded across the floor to feel my glands with warm finger-tips.

'You'll live. Had some water? A paracetamol?'

I hadn't, but I nodded.

'This is about that story, isn't it? I've been getting messages all morning.'

'Yes,' I said. 'But, I'm OK. I am.'

'Are you?'

'By this time tomorrow, everyone will have forgotten about it.'

She folded her arms. 'That's just the sort of thing

your father would say.'

'It's fine, Mum.'

She looked at me strangely for a moment, as though she was trying to decide whether or not to say something. Then: 'Adrian called. Top Music have asked if you might go in to see them, about your album.'

'Really?' I felt slightly better. No, a lot better.

A meeting, in that glass office, with the biscuits and the black-and-white photos.

And most of all, a chance to go back and agree to record that song about partying late or kittens or whatever.

Because if that's what it would take to get back into Top Music's good books, I'd do it. Those lyrics they'd shown me weren't bad, not really, and a tune was even starting to suggest itself, a fast, rumbly set of chords, leading into a—

'Katie, this isn't good for you. I'm saying this as your mother. Stop now. It's gone too far.'

'I said I'd stop when it was making me unhappy. And I'm happy! I'm really happy! I'm going to see my label. To plan my album!'

She gave me a quick kiss on the forehead. 'I'm going to bed.'

I stretched out and looked up, through my window, and into the clouds.

CHAPTER TWENTY-THREE

'Katie! Great to see you! Thanks for coming by at such short notice.'

'That's OK. It wasn't like I was doing anything else,' I said, and at the same time, Adrian said:

'Good to see you, Tony.'

We were standing in the lobby of Top Music, that glass ceiling slicing up the sunshine and throwing it down over us like liquid confetti.

'Right, let's go on up,' said Tony. 'Did you get here all right? Traffic?'

'Got the train,' said Adrian. 'You know what the M25 can be like.'

'I do,' said Tony, in what was surely one of the most boring conversations in human history. 'I always say to Emma, it's worth having a decent car; we spend enough time in it.'

'What you driving these days, Tone?'

'A Maserati – not as much fun as I'd like, but it does the job. You?'

Thank goodness I was so nervous, otherwise I'd probably have fallen asleep.

We sat down opposite Tony's enormous desk, with its clutch of leather-framed photos: Tony and a pretty blonde lady on the deck of a boat, his shirt open and his tan deeper than ever; Tony and Karamel, on the stage of what looked like *The X Factor*; and a new one of Tony being interviewed by Chris, on NTV news.

No biscuits today, I noticed.

Tony leaned forward and fixed me with his gaze.

'Well, now.'

'Mmm.'

'This is.'

'Mm?'

We seemed to have got stuck just making noises at each other. I decided to nudge things along.

'Is . . . this . . . about the last few days?' I said.

'It is,' said Tony. 'How would you say it's been going?'

I sat up. 'Right. Well, not great, obviously.'

Tony nodded, once, then twice.

'So I suppose the question is, what do we do next?' I gave him what was supposed to be my most charming smile. 'It's clear that I'm not the best person to be in control of . . . me . . . so I'm willing to do whatever you tell me to do.'

Under the table, I felt Adrian give my knee a squeeze.

We both waited.

'Katie,' said Tony. 'Katie, Katie, Katie. You are quite something, you know that?'

'Yes!'

'I've never met an artist quite like you. In fact, I've never met an artist *anything* like you.'

Adrian gave me the tiniest of winks.

'You do go your own sweet way, don't you?'

'I do!'

'Look,' said Tony. 'The problem is this. Karamel are now at number one. And your single has dropped down to ninety-four. How can I put this? People don't buy music that's based on hate. They buy out of love.'

'But . . . the iTunes chart won't include all the CD sales, will it? Adrian, you said you sold a few in the shop, and maybe other places have sold them too . . . I mean, some people still like me, right?'

'Perhaps,' said Tony. 'But a handful of CDs won't

change anything. You're not popular right now. Not with Karamel fans. And after recent *revelations*, not with Katie Cox fans, either. You're not popular with anyone.'

'Maybe not in an obvious way. But changing your mind, it's not a bad thing, it's good, really, so if I just—'

'Katie, there's no arguing with the comments.'

'But—'

Tony tapped something into his computer, and then, like he was some kind of magician or something, and this was his final show-stopping trick, swung the screen around.

There was me, at my concert, singing 'Can't Stand the Boy Band'. And underneath . . .

this is kinda mean

Katie Hater you are gonna be round for like maybe

1 month maybe too but Karamel will live 4 eva

My god this is shockingly bad and she looks AWFUL

Liar u said you hated Karamel but you love them u are full of LIES I don't trust u any more I thought u were real but u are fake like all the rest

This song, her voice and face is disgusting. How did this get released?

this song made me vomit

KRISTIAN I LOVE YOU I WILL NEVER STOP LOVING YOU

Disappointed. The whole thing is so low

She needs feeding to the sharks

Chart battle ROFL WE SLAYED YOU KATIE COX

Why is this happening? I dont understand
no no no nO

OK I'm kind of tired of this. She needs to come back to what she was when she started out

Was Katie mad when she made the video? Her eyes are mad
it started out annoying, then got bad

Her first song was pure gold this is pure poo

Last week I actually liked her now I hate her

oh dear . . .

Back then she looked and dressed so much prettier but now a days she doesn't

bad song bad attitude plus her face is MANK

download song and play in reverse it is the devil speaking

already 320k dislikes well i disliked it too

I'm crying I thought u were real Katie but you love boy bands like all the rest

Her real name is Katie Plops hahahahaa

what is going on????
Duz she hate them or luv them? Dont undertsand

am i the only one who just want to cry in sadness
because she is not who I thought

like come on

Trash music ugly girl

GO AWAY STUPID SONG

So much hate, so many people, and it kept coming, more and more and more, and all I could think was that I didn't deserve this, that no one deserved this.

And that I should have been more sympathetic to poor Nicole when she'd been trolled, back on the bus.

Back when it was all still OK.

Before the end of the world.

My vision was beginning to blur, but I wouldn't let him know, I wouldn't let my voice even betray a hint of what I was feeling as I said, 'So you think my next single should be something more positive? I can do that. I can totally do that.'

'Positive is good,' said Tony. 'And I can't wait to hear it.'

'Great!' I said. 'I'll send something over as soon as I have it. Maybe even tonight!'

'If you like,' said Tony. 'But . . . Katie, we can't release it. The album isn't going to happen. You know that, don't you?'

'I . . .' I didn't.

'No one's denying your talent, but we think perhaps you are not quite ready. For this. The music industry. You do understand.'

Such small words, but each one so heavy. Like stones thrown into deep water. Down, down, down.

'I understand,' I said.

'We've loved working with you. I'm sure our paths will cross again. When you're older.'

'Of course,' I said. 'In fact, it's sort of what I was going to say anyway.'

'Very wise,' said Tony, getting to his feet in a way that said, *Leave now, Katie, I do not want you in my office any more.*

Thank goodness for Adrian, sweeping me up in jackets and bags and a load of *let's stay in touch* and *how's Gemma, by the way*? All that middle-aged stuff that I'd never understood the point of before – I could see now that it was for moments like this. All the rubbish about property prices and the weather and trains, I suddenly understood it was like bubble wrap, or the foam pieces you get in parcels: padding out the conversation, protecting the breakable thing sitting in the middle.

The broken thing.

Me.

And all the while Adrian was talking, we were moving closer and closer to the door, and then we were in the lift, and I made sure to keep my eyes away from the mirror so that while I could feel the tears on my face, I couldn't see them, and then, finally, I was out in the street, the doors of Top Music closing behind me.

Conversational Bubble Wrap

The own-brand version tastes just fine
Have you looked it up online?
Can't stay long I have a meeting
Turn down your gas central heating

Adult talk is pointless pap
Conversational bubble wrap

Goodness me I hate this weather
They are nice are they real leather?
Want my problems I've got plenty
Detour down the A120

Adult talk, let's recap
Is conversational bubble wrap

But some days life can be too real
Sometimes I'm afraid to feel
Please don't ask me how I've been
I'd rather chat about the Queen

Fuel prices are monumental
Kids these days are going mental
Got to get back, trim our lawn
It's between the beige and fawn

But now I see my life's a trap
I think I want some bubble wrap.

CHAPTER TWENTY-FOUR

I got home to find Mum surrounded by every shoe we'd ever owned, which was a lot of shoes.

'I'm clearing out the hall cupboard,' she said, as she crawled back into the hall cupboard.

'I see,' I said. Then, to her bottom: 'Top Music, they've, er, dropped me.'

She shot out backwards. Like a champagne cork from a bottle of champagne, if the bottle was a cupboard and the cork was a bum.

'When . . . what . . . ?'

'It doesn't matter.'

She was pulling me towards her and I felt the sadness coming so I talked very fast. If I just made a wall of words then perhaps it wouldn't get through.

'I don't think I'm especially ready for any of this and performing's not really my thing.'

'I never liked that man,' said Mum.

'Me neither,' I said. 'Well, honestly, I did, then I didn't, then I wasn't sure. Then I did. And now I don't.'

'He should be protecting you,' said Mum. 'Not dropping you the second things get difficult.'

'Maybe,' I said. 'But . . . they did get difficult because of me.'

'Still,' said Mum. 'This is your chance, isn't it? To get back to normal.' She tucked a strand of hair behind my ear. 'I can't bear to see you so unhappy, Katie.'

'I'm not . . .' I began. And then, because there was no way I could even begin to pretend that I was happy about any of this: 'I'll think about it. I promise.'

She didn't say anything, but her hug told me that, finally, I was on my way to doing the right thing.

'Is there anything for dinner?' I asked her shoulder.

'Leftover Chinese,' she said. 'Top shelf of the fridge. Your father went a bit overboard last night.'

Eventually I blew my nose and went to investigate the food situation, leaving her in among a mountain of old welly boots.

I mean, I do know I should have helped or something, but there's getting back to normal and then there's clearing out the hall cupboard. I wasn't going to be *that* normal.

▶

And then I had to tell Manda.

'Just so you know,' I said, as we lay in the dark, failing to sleep. 'Just so you know, it's all over and I'm not a pop star any more because Top Music don't want me because everyone hates me. Just so you know.'

I heard her sit up. 'I saw that it was all kicking off . . . I'm sorry.'

'It's fine. I'm thinking I'm done with it all, anyway.'

We lay there, in a silence that was intense.

I think Mands must have felt it too, because she put her light on and said, 'Wanna hear something good? There's this band I found, called New York Scandal. They're these four guys from Hull; they're playing at the shop. I reckon you'll really rate them . . . their story is so inspiring . . .'

'Maybe I don't want to be inspired.'

'So, they do this brilliant riff, I've never heard anything quite like it, or maybe I have, now, come to think of it, they're almost a bit Daft Punk, in a funny kind of way, only more acoustic . . .'

And as she spoke, I saw how I'd never be free.

That music isn't just something you occasionally go and do.

That it was everywhere.

Winding itself through my family and my friendships and my laptop and my phone.

If I wanted to be free, if I wanted to be normal, then there couldn't be any more listening to gig recordings and there couldn't be any more jamming sessions. Or guitar lessons. Or new albums or karaoke, or afternoons at Vox Vinyl flicking through the racks.

Because if I did that, then the next thing was picking up my guitar, my shiny new guitar, and then I'd be writing songs and that's what got me into this horror in the first place.

If I wanted to be normal, if I wanted to be like Paige and Sofie and Savannah and Lacey, if I wanted to be *happy*, then I'd have to cut out every last little bit.

'Not tonight,' I said to Amanda.

'You're right, it's late . . .'

'And not tomorrow morning either.'

She rubbed her eyes. 'I thought you cared about this stuff, K. The shop, my gigs . . .'

'Sorry, Mands. I did. But I'm . . . just . . . finished.'

We lay there for a minute, maybe two. My head was full to overflowing with thoughts, and my stomach was just the same, only with chicken-prawn chow mein. Which reminded me.

'By the way, Dad said to give you this.' I chucked Mands the little box, which she caught, and then held. Then let slip to the floor.

'I don't want anything from him. He—'

'Gave Mum two thousand pounds.'

That got her.

'Did he?'

'Yes! Plus, he bought us a really good Chinese takeaway. There's still a bit in the fridge, I think.' Then I remembered. 'No, I finished it. But he's really trying to make things right.'

'It's not enough. He's . . .'

'Our father. And he's trying to make up for everything. I told him that he needed to start paying his way. Like you said. And he spoke to Catriona, even though he didn't want to, and he got the money back that he'd lent her for her stupid Pilates studio and he gave it to Mum.'

'Good. That's exactly what he should have done. Ages ago.'

I hesitated. But I'd come this far. 'If he can do that, can you not at least give him a chance?'

'I don't want his jewellery,' said my sister. 'And it's going to take more than a bit of money—'

'Two THOUSAND pounds! He can't do anything right, can he?'

'As far as you're concerned, he can't do anything wrong,' said Amanda, turning off the light.

So I rolled over and went to sleep. Which wasn't the easiest, given the amount of leftover Chinese food I had to digest, but I managed.

Unfortunately I then got up an hour later to drink a litre of water.

And an hour after that to have a wee.

Leftover Chinese Takeaway Blues

I'm suffering, baby
I got food remorse
Oh I'm suffering, baby
Of silver carton food remorse
I guess I should've held back
On the sweet and sour sauce

I got them blues
Got them leftover Chinese takeaway blues

Lying on my side
Feeling incredibly full
Whoah I'm lying on my side
Feeling incredibly full
I guess all I can say is
Shouldn't have had that duck spring roll

I got them blues
Got them leftover Chinese takeaway blues

Trying to sit up
In unbearable pain
Yes, trying to sit up
And I'm in the most unbearable pain
Shouldn't have finished off
All the chicken-prawn chow mein

I got them blues
Got them leftover Chinese takeaway blues

But if I could live this evening over
I know I'd do the same again.

CHAPTER TWENTY-FIVE

So, what do you know, I only woke up with the BEST idea for a song. It was called 'Leftover Chinese Takeaway Blues'. The words were ready and waiting, I had my new guitar tucked under my arm and was just getting to grips with the chords when I remembered.

No more music.

I stuck the guitar back into its case and shoved it under my bed and by the time I'd finished breakfast I'd very nearly managed to forget about it.

What was harder was fighting the need to stick my headphones in my ears and have a bit of Lana Del Ray to take me down the lane. You have to be in a very specific mood for Lana – and when you are, it's extremely important to put her on straight away before it passes.

Only, I wasn't doing music any more.

Instead, I listened to the traffic and the birds and the wind and they were just as good.

Almost as good.

They were fine.

Jaz was at the bus stop, talking to Nicole.

She didn't look at me.

'Morning,' I said.

Nicole nodded. Jaz didn't say anything at all.

I tried again. 'What's the goss?'

I don't know where I got the word 'goss'.

'We're talking about the disco,' said Jaz.

'Oooh, great! That totally fits in with my new normal life. Because I'm not a pop star any more. I'm a normal person who does stuff like going to the disco.'

'*Me and Nicole* are talking about the disco,' said Jaz, and then she turned her back on me.

Hmm.

Up in our form room, things weren't much better. Lacey was sitting deep in the Savannah Zone, and I had to battle through a wall of Prada Candy before I got to a conversation that went:

'It's the biggest shame that my boyfriend Kolin can't come to the disco. He's got this awards thing at Wembley that night. It's so annoying, but what can I do? I have to be supportive of him, because of how he's my boyfriend.'

'Hey, Lace,' I said. 'So. Disco chat! What are you going to wear? Shall we go to Oxfam?'

Lacey looked at me like I was a fly that had landed on a cream cake she'd been about to eat.

'I should think that someone like you has better places to shop.'

'No!' I had to stop myself grabbing her by the shoulders. 'I'm being normal again! Completely boring and music-free!'

'Like me,' said Lacey.

'Yes! I've given up the whole pop star thing, it wasn't exactly working out. I'm going to get back to doing ordinary person stuff. Like shopping in Oxfam. And going to the disco. You'll come with me, won't you, bestie?'

'Actually, I'm going solo,' said Lacey.

'We can still go together,' I said.

'I'm going solo with Savannah.'

'Oh. Right.'

And then, I had an idea.

'Well, that's fine, actually. You should go with Savannah. Because . . . I'm going to ask Dominic Preston!'

Going to the disco with a boy. Now that *was* normal.

'If you like,' said Lacey.

'I do like! Him! Which is why I'm going to ask him.'

268

'He's over there,' said Paige, helpfully.

'Later,' I said. This was all moving rather fast. 'I'm going to ask him later.'

'Why not now?' said Sofie.

'Because of assembly.'

'Assembly's not for ten minutes,' said Paige. 'Hey, Dom? Katie has something to ask you.'

And the four of them turned and stared at what was turning into the Katie Cox Humiliation Show.

Dominic Preston slid down off the desk and came over. He really was very good-looking. Long and lean, with nice dark eyes, and hands that looked as though they'd be smooth and warm, not wet and trembly, like mine.

'Hey, Katie. Wassup?'

'Nothing,' I said.

'But you just said you were going to—' Lacey began.

'OK. OK! Um, Dominic Preston. I wondered –' I began, before clearing my throat and starting again, a lot lower. 'I just wondered, whether you'd like to come to the disco. With someone. That someone being me.'

Those good-looking eyes blinked. 'We don't really know each other.'

'No. But . . .'

'I'm not sure the disco's exactly the place for a first date.'

'No,' I said, wanting the earth to open up and, not swallow me, because that would be terrifying, but maybe hold me for a bit until everyone had gone and then let me out again. 'No. You're right. I'm sorry. I—'

'We should go out first. Get to know each other.'

'Really?' I cleared my throat. 'That would be –' *don't seem too eager don't seem too eager* – 'fine.'

'Thursday night?'

Mum and Adrian would be at karaoke. 'Sure.'

'The Harvester OK? Seven o'clock?'

'Great!'

Then the bell rang for assembly, and I did my very best to look normal, which I completely was.

So the rest of the day unfolded in a normal way, except for not having anyone want to sit next to me in any lessons, or at lunch, and except for the bit where Jill, my guitar teacher, came to ask me why I hadn't gone to my lesson and I had to explain that I was no longer going to play the guitar, and found myself getting surprisingly upset. It didn't last beyond the end of the Double Decker that I ate to cheer myself up again, though, so that was all right.

Best of all, when I came out at half three, there, parked right across that zigzag bit that you're not supposed to stop on, was Dad!

'Hop in, darlin'.'

I hopped in.

'This is nice! How come?'

'Just thought you deserved a bit of a treat.'

'I DO,' I said. 'Everything's been so –' *don't bring things down, Katie* – 'annoying, recently.'

'Your mother said. Want to talk about it?'

'There's not much to say. I was a pop star. Now I'm not.'

'You'll always be a star to me,' said Dad.

'Great,' I said, going to turn the radio on, maybe find a bit of Jay Z to lift the mood, and then remembering I wasn't doing that any more, and folding my hands back into my lap.

'So –' Dad spun the wheel – 'when you were in there. Top Music. At the office . . . Did Tony say anything about me?'

'What?' I held my breath as we squeezed between the

two bollards on the junction, where Mands had once lost a wing mirror. 'When?'

'When you saw him. Did Tony mention my demo?'

'We didn't really get to that.'

'Oh. And you don't think you could ask?'

'Um, maybe.' I thought about it, properly. 'Actually, probably not. No.'

'Right.'

A flare of annoyance, like a match being lit. It had been pretty much the worst ten minutes of my life, in that room, and Dad had wanted me to make it about him?

Then, like always when I light matches, the feeling spluttered out again. He needed a job. I'd said I'd help him. And I hadn't.

I decided to change the subject.

'Anyway. I've got some news, Dad. I'm going on a date. My first date.'

He'd been looking thoughtful, screwing up his face in the sun, but now he sat up straight and revved the engine so hard that the driver in the van next to us gave me a funny look.

'My baby is going on her first ever date!'

'He's called Dominic Preston and he's really gorgeous.

 272

We're going to the Harvester.'

We pulled up on to the drive, and he stopped the car. 'Now, Katie, have we ever talked about the birds and the bees?'

Oh boy.

'Yes, Dad. Not you and me – but, I have had that talk.'

Thank goodness for Amanda. How people cope without big sisters, I do not know.

'Well,' said Dad, 'don't do anything that I wouldn't do.'

'Dad.'

'Anyway, I suppose there's a limit to what you can get up to in a Harvester. Although, there was this one time, in a Taco Bell, I'd just started seeing Catriona, and—'

'*DAD.*'

'Maybe I'll save that one for when you're older.'

CHAPTER TWENTY-SIX

I'd been hoping for time to do some pre-date psyching myself up, but after a full-scale disaster involving nude tights, a ladder and a bottle of red nail polish, I was running seriously late. I got off the bus to see that he was already there, standing by the door, fiddling with his phone.

He seemed different, away from school. Taller. Older.

Stay calm, I told myself. *What's the worst thing that can happen?*

My imagination immediately responded with one word:

DIARRHOEA.

'Katie! Hi!'

He saw me as I was crossing the road. I did a small wave.

'Hello, Dom. In. Ic.'

'Call me Dom?'

His voice was friendly and nice-seeming, and as I got closer, close enough to give him a sort of air kiss on the cheek and smell his deodorant, it occurred to me that I'd never had an actual conversation with the guy. I didn't know anything about him at all.

Beyond the fact that he was gorgeous, of course.

'Shall we go in?'

'I'd been thinking we could maybe sit outside,' I said, and we looked at the Harvester's picnic tables, which were lined up next to the car park and facing the very busy main road, and then up at the heavy sky. 'Nah, that was a bad thought. Let's not.'

'We can if you want?'

'No, it's fine.'

'If you want to sit outside, we should sit outside.'

'I DON'T WANT TO SIT OUTSIDE.'

He stepped backwards.

'I mean . . . inside would be lovely,' I said.

Inside was dark, with shiny red leather chairs and menus that were a bit sticky. We sat down in a table near the bar and under a speaker. The stereo was playing something catchy, but faint, and I strained to hear it above the rattle of the till.

It was . . . oh, man, it was Karamel.

The Harvester dissolved and I was standing by the

 275

side of the stage again, watching Kurt dip his head in concentration as all of the O2 screamed.

No. No, no no. This would not do. This would not do *at all*.

I needed to be focusing on Dominic Preston, who was HERE and GORGEOUS, unlike Kurt, who might have been a tiny bit good-looking and perhaps slightly talented and who seemed to really get me, BUT had sold me out to the press and not even been big enough to fess up and anyway had got the old musical Katie, not the new, normal one.

'Excuse me,' I said to the woman behind the bar. 'Is there any chance you could play something else?'

She gave me a bit of a look, then went off round the back. A second later and we were listening to Rihanna.

'So,' said Dominic Preston, smiling at me over the menu, clearly not having noticed my mini meltdown, or, if he had, being too polite to mention it. 'So.'

'So!' I said, thinking, *be normal.* 'What's your favourite food, then? Mine's roast beef. But they only do that on a Sunday. So I suppose I'll have a burger.'

'Two burgers,' said Dominic, to the woman behind the bar, and I have to say, I got a little tingle at the thought that I was on a date with someone who liked burgers as much as me, i.e. a lot.

There was a long silence. Long enough for me to clock that the stereo had stopped playing 'We Found Love' by Rihanna and started playing 'Umbrella', also by Rihanna. Long enough to count how many other people were there, which was twelve, not including waiters, and thirteen including them. Long enough to notice that time was slowing down and that the second hand on the clock above the bar was actually creaking around and I still didn't know what I was going to say and I really ought to say *something*.

Message from Katie's mouth to Katie's brain: *Hey there. Any possible conversation topics you might want to throw me here?*

Katie's brain: *Diarrhoea?*

Katie's mouth: *OK, that's great, thanks brain, thanks very much.*

'Umbrella' ended and 'Red' by Taylor Swift started up, and maybe it was just getting a bit of much-needed Tay fierceness into my ears, but I finally had the courage to stop pretending this was all fine, and say:

'Sorry, this is weird. We don't know each other at all.

 277

I shouldn't have . . . this is a bad idea. Shall I go? I'll just go. Maybe, bring my burger to school tomorrow; I'll have it cold for lunch.'

'Katie!' His hand was on mine. 'Don't . . . I know it's weird. And yeah, we don't know each other. But I've liked you for, well, forever.'

'Have you?'

He looked down at the table, and I thought how very gorgeous he was, those long eyelashes brushing his cheeks, the way his chin . . . was.

'Yeah. You must have noticed.'

'Not really. But, um, yay.'

We grinned, and everything seemed a bit better.

'So. What's it like being famous, then?'

'Oh –' I scrunched my serviette – 'I'm not doing that any more. My contract's cancelled. It's all over.'

'No!'

'Yes. But I wasn't really down with the whole celebrity thing, anyway. Let's talk about other stuff. Where do you live? Have you always been in Harltree?'

'But you're still going to get loads of money from that song you did, aren't you?'

'I don't know. So, we used to live on the other side of

Harltree, and then after my parents split up, we came to the bit by the fields in this crazy falling-down house. I hated it for ages, but now I think I maybe don't hate it quite as much as I did. Although I do still hate it. You?'

'I'm not very interesting,' said Dominic.

'Of course you are!'

'Not as interesting as you. Who's the most famous person you've ever met?'

The answer was obviously Kurt, but I wasn't going to say that, obviously. 'I chatted to Crystal Skye for a bit at a thing, but it wasn't really that exciting.'

Our burgers arrived, which was good, because I really like burgers. He didn't seem particularly keen on his. After about three minutes of frenzied eating on my side of the table and a bit of poking around on his, I said:

'Not hungry?'

'I'm all right.'

'Because this is really good,' I said, managing to squirt burger juice down my front. 'Go on. Have a bit.'

'I'm . . . I'm sort of . . . a vegetarian,' said Dominic.

'Oh. You could go to the salad bar, if you want, I think it comes free with any main course.'

'Are you going?'

I laughed so loudly that an old man at the bar gave me a look. 'I'm not really a salad person.'

'Then I'm fine,' said Dominic.

'Why did you order a burger?'

'Because you did.'

'Er, OK.'

Was that an odd thing to do? This is the problem with first dates. You don't have anything to compare them to.

Maybe it wasn't odd. Maybe it was nice. After all, he was smiling at me, and saying:

'You're really cool, Katie.'

'Am I? I mean, thank you. So, anyway, what sort of music do you like?'

He put his chin into his cupped hand and smiled. '*Your* music.'

No, this definitely was a bit weird. But, a good kind of weird. Definitely the good kind. 'Thanks!' I said. 'But, other than that?'

'Oh, you know.'

I'd finished my burger, and was now down to the last few chips. Dominic had barely touched his. Not even the chips. Not even the chips that weren't touching the burger. He was just watching me, with an intense expression.

Maybe this was chemistry.

'I don't!' I said. Perhaps he was just shy. 'Look, OK. So, I'm majorly into Joni Mitchell at the moment, and Adele, I know she's everywhere, but it's totally justified, she's this incredible talent, isn't she? And Feist, and Amy Winehouse, she only made two albums, but they're so perfect. Have you ever heard any Ella Fitzgerald? The way she sings, it gives me chills. And Billie Holiday, obviously. Lorde's pretty cool. And Caitlin Rose. And . . .' I was talking far too much. 'OK, now you say someone.'

He coughed. 'I . . . suppose . . . I like . . . the Beatles.'

'Yes! Me too! Which is your favourite album? Mine's probably the White Album but I'm majorly into their earlier stuff too.'

'I like *Dark Side of the Moon*.'

'See, that's not actually a Beatles album,' I said. 'It's by Pink Floyd. But it is really good; I absolutely get why you'd choose it.'

'Katie, will you go out with me?'

And there it was.

Normal life!

I'd be Dominic Preston's girlfriend!

We'd go to the disco together, and hang out, and

listen to *Dark Side of the Moon*.

'Yes! That would be nice.'

We linked hands across the table, and I hoped that he didn't mind mine being a bit sticky and smelling of meat.

'And now, when you do concerts and stuff I can come with you!'

'Yeah,' I said. 'Except I've given that up. Like I said – um, sorry, what are you doing?'

He had his phone up in the air. 'Just taking a photo.'

'Great. Why?'

'To show everyone. Because you're my girlfriend.'

'Because I'm your girlfriend,' I said, trying not to flinch as he took one, then three, then five photos, some of me, some of me and him, one of me and my empty plate. 'Cool.'

'So, we should plan another date. Me and my celebrity girlfriend.'

'Yes,' I said, wondering why it was that another date with Dominic Preston wasn't sounding nearly as exciting as it would have done even half an hour ago. 'But, look. I'm not this celebrity. I'm just like you, like everyone else at school. That's OK, isn't it?'

A new waitress had come to take our plates, and as

she did, she gave me a double take. 'Aren't you . . . ?'

'She's Katie Cox,' said Dominic. 'The one who got all those hits on her video. She had a number two single.'

'Oh wow,' said the waitress. 'Will you sign . . . will you sign –' She looked around for something for me to sign. There wasn't anything. Even the menus were laminated – 'My pad! Will you sign my pad?'

'I don't want to,' I said. 'I mean, I can, but I'm trying not to do that sort of thing. Sorry.'

She took a step back. 'I see. Think you're too good for this, do you?'

'No! It's just . . .'

'I'll get your bill.' And she stomped off.

I was almost too shocked to cry. Almost. The tears wobbled on my lashes as I said, 'Sorry, was that . . . ? I only said that I didn't want to . . .'

'I suppose that means you won't sign this, either,' said Dominic, sliding a CD out of his pocket. It was 'Just Me', still in its wrapper.

'I'd rather not,' I said.

The bill came smacking down on to the table. I got out a tenner. He didn't move.

'Aren't you . . . this is all I have . . .'

'But you can afford to pay it,' he said.

'I can't, especially. At least, not tonight.'

Finally, he got his wallet out and put down a ten-pound note too. And then we were going out, past the horrible waitress, watching me like I was made of solidified puke or something, and into the car park.

'Well, this has been –'

He was looking at me funny.

'Really great, and everything. And –'

He was leaning in.

'And I'm so glad we did it, but –'

He was close now, so close, because, oh man, he was about to kiss me. Either that or he was examining my earrings.

No, he was tilting his head, and I could feel his breath, in fact, I could even smell it. This was definitely pre-kiss territory. I was about to experience my very first kiss. And –

'I'm sorry,' I said. 'I'm not sure I'm . . . that we're . . . I'm sorry.'

He took a step back, and half closed his eyes. Eyes that somehow didn't seem nearly as gorgeous as they had. 'Is it because you only fancy celebrities now?'

'No! Just—'

'That waitress was right, back there. I'm not good enough for you. None of this is good enough for you.'

'No! That's not what . . . no!'

'Get lost, Katie Cox.'

CHAPTER TWENTY-SEVEN

But . . .

But but but but but . . .

But . . .

My mouth formed the word, over and over again, only before I could finish, he'd gone.

Even if he'd stayed, I don't know what I would have said.

He'd looked at me, the waitress had looked at me, and what had they seen? Not me, or at least, not the real me.

They'd seen a version of Katie Cox, the girl who sang and played and grinned into her webcam. They hadn't seen the me who wanted to disappear.

My hand went for my phone.

Manda didn't pick up.

Mum didn't pick up.

Adrian didn't pick up.

Dad didn't even have his switched on.

Lacey, she screened me. I could tell because it rang five times. Just long enough for her to see who it was and hit ignore. So cruel. She could at least have let it go to voicemail *naturally*.

I didn't even stop to think about the last person I'd dialled until I heard her voice saying:

'What?'

'Um, hi, Jaz.'

'Go away.'

'OK!' I put the phone down.

It began to drizzle.

I redialled.

'What?'

'Jaz, I—'

'I told you to go away.'

'All right.' I hung up again.

The rain was really coming down now.

'WHAT?'

'Jaz, can we do this face to face? I'm worried water's going to get into my phone and it's not insured.'

Jaz, it turned out, lived two roads across from me, which was a forty-five-minute walk from the Harvester, minimum. And I was wearing my red sandals – sandals that completely broke my usual shoe rule, which is that all footwear needs to be good for at least an hour's standing slash walking.

And all for Dominic Preston, who clearly hadn't noticed them.

In fact, I thought, as I made my way towards the underpass, I don't think he'd noticed actual me at all.

So Dominic Preston was now officially off the radar. But that was all right. That still left loads of other people who liked the real, normal me.

People like . . .

People like . . .

People like the people on the internet. Who thought I was stupid and manky and ugly and wrong. People who wanted me wiped off the face of the earth. On my phone and in my laptop and serving at the Harvester and in my class and going on a date and I'd never be safe, never get to be just me ever again.

A sob tore at my throat.

In my head, Mum's voice: 'Calm down, Katie. Calm down.'

I'd been too ambitious, that was all. Obviously it would take longer than a couple of days to undo everything that had happened. The new normal Katie would come. I was just going to have to work a bit harder, that was all. Harder on . . . what, exactly?

What would normal Katie Cox do?

Watch TV, do a bit of messaging; tidying my room was pretty much a full-time job. I could do that. And let my thoughts flit away. There was really no need to capture them in my lyric book any more. It wouldn't help.

The music, though. Just talking about the White Album back there had made my ears thirst for 'While My Guitar Gently Weeps'.

And Billy Joel! How would I live without Billy Joel? Or Jimi Hendrix? Or Dolly Parton or Amy Winehouse or Miles Davis? If there was ever a walk that needed the soundtrack of *Kind of Blue*, it was this one.

It was only now that I began to wonder. I could just about live without music for a day, even two. But those voices, the voices of my deepest feelings, the voices – even though I'd never meet them – of my friends . . . I'd have to live without them forever.

When I'd pictured Jaz's house, it was pretty much exactly like the castle in *Dracula*. High on a hill, with turrets and bats, and in the centre of a red, red room, a coffin, and in that coffin, Jaz.

Not a semi-detached with a porch and a stained-glass front door, opened by smiling, plumpish woman with dyed blonde hair who said:

'Jasmine's in her bedroom, upstairs, second door on the right.'

'OK,' I said, putting my head down and heading for the stairs.

'It's great to meet you, Katie. Jasmine's always talking about you. She's really changed since the two of you've been friends, you know. Come out of herself. We're so glad she found you.'

'Er, yeah,' I said.

I'd not been expecting that, either. Nor a beige carpet and a mishmash of framed pictures going up the stairs; baby Jaz, Jaz on a tricycle. Jaz in a bridesmaid's dress, smiling with gappy teeth.

Luckily, I opened her bedroom door on to what was basically a shrine to Marilyn Manson, and saw Jaz scowling from somewhere in the middle of a black lace hooded dress thing covered in diamanté grim reapers.

Phew.

'I've ruined my life,' I informed her. 'And now I'm paying for it, and I deserve it, I know I do, but I don't think I can bear much more.'

'You do deserve it,' said Jaz.

'Oh, Jaz. I should never have accused you of selling that story. It's not your style.'

'No. It's not.'

'I mean,' I said, wanting her to understand, 'you are quite mad. But—'

'I don't lie,' said Jaz. 'I don't lie about what I believe.'

'No,' I said. 'And from now on, I'm not going to, either.' She didn't seem convinced. 'Jaz, please. I'll give up Lacey and Karamel. But I cannot lose you too. You're amazing. I wish I could be more like you.'

And, blow me down, but were those *tears* I saw in her eyes?

'Enough melodrama.' She pushed back her hair and I realized I must have been mistaken. Eyes like Jaz's couldn't possibly cry. If nothing else, they were surely too blocked up with kohl. 'Drippy Lacey will come sliming back. And you love Karamel.'

'I do not love them. I mean, I love their music. Loved it. But . . . Kurt sold me out. He said he'd forgiven me and then he went to the press.'

Jaz chewed, possibly a piece of gum, possibly just a

complicated thought. 'Maybe not,' she said. 'Have you at least considered that it was someone else?'

'No! It was him. Of course it was him.'

'Then let's start by doing that. Who else was there? Who saw you? At the concert?'

'Um. That journalist, Chris.'

'It's a good story; he'd have reported it, with his name. So it's not him.'

'There were loads of backstage people. It could have been any of them.'

'They'd have signed stuff saying they wouldn't talk to the press. It's not going to be one of them.'

'It has to be. Because the only other person is Dad, and it's not him.'

'Why not?' asked Jaz.

'Because Dad wouldn't do that! He's not . . . he just wouldn't. OK?' I wasn't convincing her. 'He's my *dad*.'

'Kurt from Karamel's dad sold stories about him,' said Jaz. 'There's loads of stuff floating around out there. Some people say that's what their second album's all about.'

'How did you know that?' I asked. 'And since when have you been into Karamel?'

'Couple of weeks,' said Jaz. 'But we're talking about you. And your dad.'

'Look,' I said. 'Dad's had a few . . . issues. But we're talking about a man who gave Mum two thousand pounds a few days ago. And it's not like he can exactly afford it.'

Jaz leaned forward. 'If he can't afford it, then where did he get two grand? From Pop Trash?'

'No! From Catriona. His ex-girlfriend. He loaned her some money, we had a talk, he got it back and gave it to Mum.'

Jaz nodded at my phone. 'Easy enough way to check,' she said.

'I trust him,' I said. 'I am not phoning Catriona.'

Jaz didn't reply. And I looked at my phone and pictured Dad's face, felt his arms around my shoulders, and I knew – one hundred per cent knew – that he hadn't . . . this was Dad we were talking about . . .

I also knew what Amanda would say.

Exactly what Amanda would say.

And that Amanda was wrong.

'If you know it wasn't him, if that's genuinely what you believe, then fine,' said Jaz, and she looked as serious as I've ever seen her. 'But if any part of you believes that it

 293

might have been him, then . . . You said you were going to tell the truth from now on, Katie. You just told me that.'

'I . . . I don't have her number,' I said. 'She could be anyone. Her and Dad have split up, and I can't ask him, can I?'

'What do you know about her?'

'Nothing helpful. That she runs a Pilates studio in California. That her surname is something like Fernando or Ferdinand or—'

'Catriona Fernandez,' said Jaz, looking triumphantly up from her phone. 'Here's the number for her studio.'

'But suppose it's the middle of the night over there? Suppose she doesn't want to speak to me. Or she's in the middle of teaching a class. Suppose –' and then I had to stop talking because Jaz was shoving her phone to my ear and I could hear ringing. And then:

'Poise Pilates, can I help you?'

'Um. Hi. I was just wondering if I could speak to Catriona only she's probably not there so never mind I'll just—'

'Speaking. How may I help you?' She sounded very American. Like she was in a film or something. I thought, not for the first time recently, that my life didn't seem real any more.

'Oh. This is . . . um . . . Katie. Katie Cox. Benjamin Cox's daughter. Sorry.'

'You Brits, always apologizing. Hi there, Katie! Great to finally speak to you. How is Benji?'

'He's, er, OK.'

'I'm so glad! He's a good guy, you know? Of course you do, he's your dad! And how can I help you, Katie?'

Jaz was looking at me, very, very hard, as I said, 'Sorry. I mean, not sorry. But, this is a bit . . .' Jaz tilted her head. 'Did Dad lend you some money?'

'He sure did, honey. I never asked, you know that? But he saw I needed a little help, and when the studio lease came up, there he was with the down payment. He's a generous guy.'

I began to smile. It was all going to be OK. 'He *is* generous, isn't he?'

'Didn't even ask for it back when we split.'

'No?' My stomach began to turn.

'Nope! Not a single dollar. But I'm going to return every dime. The second we start turning a profit, I'm setting up a standing order. My mamma told me, Catriona, you don't ever stay in debt. Especially not to a man.'

 295

'Huh,' I said.

'Oh, I'm so glad to be able to talk to you, Katie. Your dad, he was always so proud of you. Showing everyone your photo, telling anyone who'd listen about his baby girl. He loves you so much.'

'Yeah,' I said. 'Um, I have to go now, Catriona.'

'Send him my love, will you?'

'I will.'

'Bye bye, honey pie.'

I let the phone drop on to Jaz's bed.

'That doesn't mean he did it,' I said. 'He could have got the money anywhere. Maybe it was from work. An old job! He's always saying how they take forever to pay up. Maybe . . . maybe . . . oh no . . . no no no . . .'

'Stay there,' said Jaz. 'I'll get Mum to drive you home.'

It doesn't mean . . .

Just because he didn't . . .

He's not . . .

The house was empty. Everyone was out. Everyone except—

'Dad?'

He had the fridge open, and when he heard my voice,

he turned, his face bathed with a sickly yellow light. 'Katie!' My eyes must have given away some of what I was feeling, because he peered at me, and said, 'What?'

'Dad. That story about me at the Karamel concert. That's . . . everywhere. Did it . . . did it come from you?'

Please. Please say no.

Please say something.

Please.

'D-Dad?'

His silence said it all.

'How could you, Dad? How *could* you?'

'I was out of cash; you were saying your mother needed rent.'

'So, couldn't you, I don't know, get a job or something?'

'It's not . . . Phone's not been ringing much recently. Haven't had a dry spell like this in a while.' He looked up. 'Don't suppose you had a chance to speak to Tony, did you?'

Dad's never been especially good at reading a situation. This, though, this took things to a whole new level.

'A few days in the studio would sort things out, see if you can't get me in, will you?'

'Dad, you sold a story about me!'

'They only wanted a chat, about you and what you were up to, it was such a great evening, where's the harm?'

'WHERE'S THE HARM? Don't you even . . . I mean, it was a Karamel concert . . . I wasn't supposed to be having a good time.'

'Weren't you? Then why were we there?'

'Dad, have you got any idea of what's been going on these last few days? With my life? Any idea at all?'

'Don't you like your new guitar?'

'Of course, but I . . .'

'Because I remembered,' he said, like some kitten I was kicking in the face. 'You said that was the guitar you wanted.'

'*That's* what you took from the concert? You knew what I had to say about Karamel and you went off and sold me out and you think you can make it OK with a poxy new guitar? Didn't . . . didn't you even hear my song?'

'Of course I did! I loved it! I'm so proud of you.'

And, oh, a part of me still thrilled to hear him say it.

'You shouldn't have done it, Dad.'

'I couldn't live off that man's charity.'

'But, why didn't you ask for the money back from Catriona?'

He looked away. 'Allow a man a bit of dignity, Katie.'

Then, in a single beat, I hated him.

'And you let me blame poor Kurt,' I said. 'You let me go online and tell the whole world it was him, when all the time it was you?'

He was laughing now. '*Poor Kurt*? I'm not going to feel too sorry for him, thank you very much!'

I thought I might . . . I don't even know. Punch a wall or be sick. Because Amanda was right. She'd been right from the start.

'Katie? Katie!'

'I thought you cared about me,' I said. 'I thought I mattered. But you only care about you.'

My voice must have cracked or something, because he stopped laughing.

'These past few weeks, I've been defending you! To Mum, to Amanda . . . It's like, you destroyed the family once and now you're coming back to do it all over again.'

I thought he'd deny it. Instead, he bowed his head. 'That's fair,' he said. 'I let you all down. I know that.'

'If you know that, then why did you . . . ?'

299

'I let you down,' he repeated. 'If I could go back and do things differently, then I would. But I can't.'

I was backing away from him now, knowing that I couldn't breathe even a molecule of air that had passed through his lungs.

'Katie, how do you think it feels, to have to go begging to your daughter? Can we not just . . .'

'No,' I said. 'In fact . . .' I got out my phone.

Hi Tony

It's Katie. So, I lied to you, about Dad being unreliable, because I didn't want him to go away. But if there's still a job on that Papaya album, you should give it to him. I reckon you owe me that. I won't bother you again.

Katie

'There,' I said. 'I've got you some work. With Tony.'

'I – I don't know what to say.'

I did. 'Go to America. And this time, don't come back.'

CHAPTER TWENTY-EIGHT

Mands found me sitting on the floor. I don't know what time it was, but it must have been late. It was dark outside, and when she came past me I could smell the night air in her hair.

I say 'found'. What I mean is that she tripped over my right arm and went flying.

'What on earth are you doing there?'

'Sorry. I was just … Sorry.' I rubbed my elbow. 'Where've you been?'

'Since when do you care?'

She snapped the light on and I had to shield my eyes. 'Wuh?'

She took her jacket off, angrily, and sat down on her bed. 'You're the one who's completely wrapped up in her own little world. "Oh, I'm a pop star, I'm dating, I'm hanging out with Super Dad . . ." What? Why are you looking at me like that?'

'It was Dad,' I said. 'Not Kurt. It was Dad. He sold me out. For money. It was always Dad.'

She tensed. Then, 'Of course it was. Oh, Katie.'

Then she held me while I cried. It was a long time.

She didn't say, 'I told you so'. She didn't remind me how Dad had ducked out of coming to see me sing solo at the school carol concert when I was nine because he'd got a last-minute spot on Jools Holland. She didn't mention that, three years ago, he'd set his heart on a vintage guitar, a handmade Benedetto Fratello, and in order to buy it, sold our car. And she didn't say anything about how he'd been too much of a wuss to tell Mum he was coming back, how he'd left it to me, and then sold me out and ruined everything.

Or perhaps it was already ruined, and I just hadn't noticed.

Funny how it takes being pressed face first into a denim jacket to get a bit of perspective on things.

Finally, Manda spoke. 'I've got a Yorkie in my bag.'

'A raisin one?' My voice sounded weird. Croaky and soft. Like someone else's.

'A raisin one, yes. You never change, you know that, Katie?'

We shared it out, and I felt, not better, exactly, but at least stable.

'Everyone hates me,' I said.

'You're being absurd.'

'I'm not. Dominic Preston just told me to get lost. Kurt blocked me. Lacey called me a liar.' I picked up the charm bracelet, then let the cold metal slip between my fingers, back on to my bedside table. 'I *am* a liar.'

'OK, but . . .'

'And the only people who hate me more than Karamel fans are the Katie Cox fans. Ex-fans.' I put my head in my hands. 'Maybe I need a new identity. Do you think I qualify for a witness protection programme? Or a new face?'

For a second, I thought how, actually, a new face might be quite nice, how I could maybe get a smaller nose, one of those ski-slope ones like Savannah has, and properly white teeth.

I could ask them to make my eyes not look quite so much like Dad's too.

'What I don't understand is where all this hate came from in the first place,' said Amanda.

Wasn't it obvious?

'It's music,' I said. 'Music keeps people apart. It divides people. That's what it does.'

'No, it doesn't.'

'It does! That's what I've realized, you see. That's where

everything started. If it hadn't been for music, I'd still be mates with Lacey, I wouldn't have the entire population of the universe wanting to kill me, and Mum and Dad would probably still be together!'

Amanda shook her head. 'That is the biggest load of rubbish I've ever heard.'

What?

'What?'

'Of course it's not music's fault. Music is –' her face worked as she struggled to get her feelings into words – 'music is the best thing. It's the only thing. It's everything.'

' . . . No.'

She went to the stereo and put on Irma Thomas, 'Good Things Don't Come Easy'. Her voice filled the room, filled up my heart. For ages, we just listened.

'I thought, if I just stopped playing, that would be enough,' I said into the thick silence that followed. 'It's over. So why isn't it over?'

'Because it isn't,' said Amanda.

Somehow, I knew that she was right.

'OK then,' said Jaz.

It was the next morning, and the Katie Emergency

Committee – i.e. the very few people in the world who could still bear to look at me – was sitting around the table having breakfast.

The fact that we were there at 8 a.m. just goes to show what an emergency it was.

Adrian cleared his throat, this long, flappily wet noise that made me remember that I'm never going to smoke, and said, 'What can we do?'

'*We* can't do anything,' said Amanda.

'What can we do to help?'

'Nothing,' I said. 'The entire world thinks I'm a complete idiot and they're right. I can't get near Lacey, and even if I could, what am I going to say to her? Plus, I accused Kurt . . .' I couldn't even finish that one.

'So tell him who it really was,' said Amanda. 'And that you're sorry.'

'I should.' Then I thought about it for more than half a second, and plunged even further into my pit of despair. 'But I can't. There's no way.'

'That one seems easy enough to sort out.' Adrian took a glug of cold coffee. 'Can't you just send him a message? Through one of your websites?'

'No,' I told him. 'He blocked me.'

'Are you sure?'

I unlocked my phone and scrolled through, but there was no Kurt. Instead, I just got a load of Paige and Sofie and Lacey, banging on about getting a pre-disco manicure, and how orange was the colour to go for because of how it went with everything or didn't go with anything or something. They were getting loads of likes, so clearly some people were finding it useful.

'He's gone,' I said. 'And anyway, I think maybe this is one of those conversations it's better to have in private. If I told him online, it would be like I was saying it just so that everyone else could hear.'

'You'll have to stalk him,' said Jaz. 'Go to a concert. Turn up in his dressing room. You're still famous enough for them to let you in.'

I put my phone back down on the table. If Lacey wanted to paint her fingers a colour called Satsuma Sunset, that was her business. 'I can't turn up at a Karamel concert. They'll eat me.'

I waited for someone to disagree, to tell me that I was being over the top, that it would be fine. No one did.

'Anyway their tour's over. They're not playing in the UK again. Not for I don't know how long.'

'They are,' said Jaz, looking at her screen. 'They're playing tonight, at the Teen Time Awards.'

Which rang a bell, somewhere at the back of my head. 'The Teen Time Awards. That's at . . .'

'Wembley,' said Amanda. 'So we have to go to Wembley. For six o'clock. Oh DAMN.'

'What?'

'It's gig night at the shop. But you know what? I'll cancel. If forty people wanted to come tonight, they'll want to come again next week.'

'Forty? So we're sold out?' said Adrian, and I remembered all over again how hard he and Amanda had worked to make that place a success. And how I'd told her that I didn't care about the shop. Or her gigs. Great stuff, Katie.

'Yeah, it's been sold out since yesterday,' said Mands. 'But you're more important.'

'No,' I said, suddenly desperate. 'I'm not. You've got to run the gig. But . . . I'll miss you.'

'I should hope so,' said my annoying, sanctimonious, *brilliant* big sister.

' . . . OK.'

'So you have to go to Wembley Arena, and go

 307

backstage and then get into Kurt's dressing room.' She made it sound as easy as a trip to Asda.

'Er, how?'

'Can't your record label . . . ?' began Jaz.

'No, they dropped me.'

'So find another way.'

'Give up, Jaz. It's impossible.' I flicked my phone on again, to see Paige's face beaming next to a large and sparkly shoe.

'We need some kind of connection,' said Amanda. 'A way into the band.'

'But there isn't one!' I refreshed, and got a picture of a Prada label, next to a sad face emoji, and the words, '*Sooo upset I have to go to the disco tonight without my beautiful boyfriend.*'

'Will you please put your phones away?' said Adrian. 'It's like talking to a pair of zombies! Honestly, when I was your age . . .'

'I know,' said Amanda. 'You wouldn't think this was something they cared about, would you? Hold on. What? What is it?'

My eyes met Jaz's.

'Savannah.'

CHAPTER TWENTY-NINE

I had to wait outside the manicure place for what felt like forever. Then, just as I was about to give up and go crawl into bed and never come out, they all turned together, wibbling a bit on the cobbles because even Lacey had stuck her heels on early. Which, if you ask me was a major error with the whole disco still to go, but let's be clear, literally no one was asking me.

Then, they saw me, and stopped.

My hand was in my pocket, so Lacey couldn't see the charm bracelet. It was there, though, around my wrist, reminding me that I'd once had a best friend.

'Hello, Savannah!' I sang, trying to appear as carefree as possible. 'Afternoon, Sofie, hey Lace, hi Paige! You look nice. I like your . . . skin.'

'Thanks, Katie,' said Paige, who in fact does have very good skin, although it wasn't looking much different from how it normally did.

'What are you even doing here, babes?' said Savannah. 'This is a *beauty* salon.'

'I know. But I was thinking about what you said. About how I'm rotten to the core and stuff and I thought maybe, if I got a bit more graceful and pretty, it might make me a better person. You know?'

I could barely make sense of what was coming out of my own mouth. Only then, Savannah nodded, very seriously, and said:

'Perhaps. You know what they say. Beauty starts on the outside.'

I moved between her and the door.

'So here's the thing, Sav. I just found out that I won a bag.'

'That's great, babes. But I'm going to be late for my nail appointment. So—'

'A designer bag. By, er, Gucci.'

She stopped, and stood a little straighter. I was reminded of how tigers go when they see baby gazelles. Yes, Savannah was practically sniffing the air.

'It's so random,' I went on. 'I entered this competition forever ago, one of those email ones, you know. And the next thing I know, this delivery guy is knocking on the door with a Gucci bag!'

'Uh huh.' She was leaning in.

'And here's the thing,' I said. '*I don't even like it!*'

'That is understandable,' said Savannah. 'You are not really a Gucci kind of a girl, Katie. And that bag, it deserves a Gucci kind of a girl.'

'Exactly,' I said. 'So I was wondering, could you come and have a look at it? Tell me what to do? Maybe you know someone who might like it . . . ?' I glanced around. 'I mean, I don't want to make you late for your disco preparations.'

'No, that's fine. This is important. Paige? Sof? You'll go ahead and explain, mmm?'

They went.

But Lacey – Lacey did not go.

Lacey stayed put. And said:

'What competition?'

'Oh, you know.'

'Because I don't remember you entering an email competition to win a Gucci bag. You say that those competitions are pointless. And you hate designer stuff.'

The bracelet was starting to feel like a handcuff or something. I could literally feel my cheeks starting to heat up as I said, 'I know! It was a complete mistake, actually, that's what makes it so surprising that I won! Go

311

get your manicure, Lacey. I don't want to make *you* late as well!'

'Where is this bag?' said Savannah.

'I left it in the car. Just round the corner. It won't take a sec.'

'Something is going on,' said Lacey.

Savannah looked from me to Lacey and back again. I did my very best to seem completely casual and like I'd accidentally won a nasty-looking Gucci bag. There isn't an obvious face for that. But—

'OK,' said Savannah. 'Show me.'

'This way,' I said, and motioned her around the corner, where Adrian was sitting in the car with the engine going and the back door open.

Savannah said, 'It's in here, yes, yes?'

'In the back, that's right,' I said, getting behind her as she leaned in and then, with just one tiny push on her perfect backside she fell forward and Jaz rose up from the foot well and pulled her down, and I hurled in behind her and slammed the door, and Adrian revved the engine and then we were off, zooming down the main road, and we'd done it, sort of. We'd . . .

'KIDNAPPED ME!' gasped Savannah.

Just as Lacey turned around from the front seat and said:

'Katie, what are you *doing*?'

It took quite a long time to explain, partly because Savannah kept screaming.

'So, basically, I need to get backstage at the Teen Time Awards.'

'Eeeeeeeeeew! This seat fabric is so ICKY!'

'Because I have to apologize to Kurt and this is the last chance I'll ever get.'

'What is ON THIS SEATBELT?'

'And I know everything is ruined and my life is over, but I thought, if I could make this one thing right . . .'

'JAZ IS LOOKING AT ME. MAKE HER STOP LOOKING.'

'Jaz, stop looking at Savannah.'

'You know this really *is* kidnap,' said Lacey. 'I could phone the police.'

I saw Adrian's hands stiffen on the steering wheel.

'Well, you're not kidnapped, Lace. You chose to get in. But, I suppose, yeah. If you wanted to, you could.'

And Savannah said, 'Where is the bag, please?'

Lacey's groan filled the car. 'There isn't a bag,

Savannah. It was a way to get you in here. They're using you. To force their way into Karamel's dressing room. They're exploiting your relationship with Kolin.'

'But I don't even have a relationship with Kolin,' said Savannah.

'What?'

The car began to slow. Along with my pulse.

'You said . . .' My voice cracked. 'You kept talking about how Kolin was your boyfriend.'

Savannah was silent.

'Sav?' Lacey leaned around the seat, looking as shocked as I've ever seen her. 'Are you all right?'

'Fine, thanks, Lacey,' said Savannah, and, OMG, the girl was on the verge of crying.

'Do you want some water?' I said, scrabbling in my bag. 'Or, here – I've got a Mars Milk.'

She looked like she was going to throw it back in my face, only then, miracle of miracles, she opened it and took a sip. And did this kind of ecstatic groan.

'What is this?'

'It's a Mars Milk.'

'I've never . . . it tastes like . . .'

'Calories. That's what calories taste like.'

She took a long swig, and then another. And another.

'Er, Sav. You and Kolin . . . ?'

She blinked, her eyes deep blue beneath twin pools of tears. 'He did text me. He texted me a lot. We texted for ages. Only . . .'

'What?' said Lacey, and she gave Savannah this sweet, kind smile, and I thought, Sav has a heart. How did I miss this?

'Only then he said he wanted to meet up. And so I stopped texting him back.'

'Why the . . . ?' I started. Then, after Lacey shot me a glare: 'Um, I mean, I'm sure you had a very good reason, but . . . why?!'

Another long swig. 'Because . . . I'm not you, Katie.'

'No. You're way better than me.'

'I'm way better *looking* than you,' corrected Savannah. 'But I'm not . . . I don't have any . . . talent. I'm just a pretty girl. Like everyone else. Well, prettier than everyone else. But that's it.' She sniffed. 'Kolin would have found out and . . . you may be facially challenged, Katie, but at least you're . . . original.'

Savannah was insecure?

Savannah was jealous of *me*?

Genuinely, I don't know anything about anything.

'Savannah,' I said, 'you are completely original. I've never met anyone like you. You're beautiful—'

'I know,' said Savannah.

'I mean, inside. You're really funny. Often without realizing it, but hey. Plus, you've been a great friend to Lacey recently. Which is more than can be said for me.'

Lacey shifted in her seat.

'In fact,' I went on, 'I'd say, as far as friends went, I'm pretty much the worst there is.'

There was a long pause.

My eyes met Lacey's in the mirror.

'But I can't,' said Savannah. 'I never texted him back. I can't just suddenly get in contact now. What will he think of me? Don't ask any more, Katie, I won't do it. And nothing you can say will change my mind.'

Then Adrian said:

'If you get us into Karamel's dressing room, Savannah, I'll buy you a Gucci bag.'

'Total yes,' said Savannah.

That conversation happened in the first part of the car journey, but in fact it was another forty-five minutes before we got to Wembley. Forty-five minutes is quite a long time even in a normal situation. Forty-five minutes in a car with a silent ex-best friend, a scary person and a Savannah is actual forever.

Lacey had her head down and wasn't saying much, which was like having a black hole sitting on the front seat, sucking up every scrap of small talk any of the rest of us managed to generate and making it disappear.

Savannah was scrolling through Gucci bags on her phone.

'Maybe a tote? But, hmm, a waste to get canvas, it won't wear well. I think it has to be leather, yes? Oooh, this one's nice. It's cross body and the G's are embossed.'

'How much?' said Adrian.

'Eight hundred and fifty.'

The car swerved and we nearly went into the central barrier.

'You had to say a Gucci bag, didn't you, Katie,' said Adrian. 'It couldn't just be Topshop.'

'Topshop is OK,' said Savannah.

'Great! In that case—'

'For other girls.'

'Right.'

'In fact, might we consider upgrading to Prada?'

'No.'

'Look,' I said. 'We don't have to do this. It's not like it's the answer to all of my problems. It's not even the answer to some of my problems.' I thought, and sighed. 'It's the answer to one of my problems. One of many. And that's if he even . . .'

Then, on the horizon, I saw it. That arch.

Wembley.

'So here's what we need to do. All very simple, nothing to get in a panic about,' said Adrian, looking rather grey. 'We've got to get through security and go backstage. And we mustn't let anyone see Katie. And I don't want to get the car towed, so some kind of permit might be nice.'

We all looked at Savannah. Who said, 'GG supreme mini chain bag. In a blossom finish. Six hundred is a bargain, really.'

Swallowing very hard, Adrian nodded, and Savannah lifted her phone to her ear. 'Kolin! It's Sav. From the party. I know, I did mean to call . . . Were you? Were you? Oh, Kolin. You are very sweet.'

This went on for a very long time.

'Aw.'

And on.

'Squee!'

And on.

Finally, about a year later, I tapped on my watch. Which Savannah looked at, and wrinkled her nose.

'Eew. No, not you! I just saw the most revolting timepiece.'

'*Savannah!*'

'So, here's the thing. I'm actually outside Wembley, right now . . . complete coincidence . . . yes . . . oh I know . . . of course, babes . . .'

It wasn't working. He was surely telling her to go away. Because, now that I thought about it properly, obviously you don't meet up with people you ran into once at a party just before you sing to Wembley Arena. I mean, if you're me, you're too busy puking to even think of using your mouth for anything else.

Only, then . . .

'Yay! So we're in this completely grim, like, truck thing, it's blue, I know, it does go with my eyes, thank you, will you tell the security people? See you in five. Kiss kiss.'

'Thank you, Savannah,' said Adrian. 'Now, Katie, it's up to you.'

CHAPTER THIRTY

I'm not going to go into the Savannah/Kolin reunion, which involved the two of them gluing their faces together with Savannah's Crème de la Mer lip balm, while me, Lacey, Jaz and Adrian stood and admired the wall.

Eventually, after about a hundred thousand years of whispers and giggles, Savannah pointed and said, 'Dressing room seven. He's on his own; Kristian went to find something to eat.' And then she went back to kissing Kolin.

Adrian turned to Jaz and Lacey.

'Shall we . . . go and find a cup of tea?'

'OK,' said Lacey.

'No way, I want to see this. I mean, yeah, all right,' said Jaz.

I took a deep breath. And wondered what the point of taking a deep breath was, as it never seemed to help.

Then I knocked, and went inside.

▶

I guess I'd been expecting Karamel's dressing room to be this kind of deluxe palace of gorgeousness with, I don't know, gold walls and a jacuzzi. Instead, it was just quite nice, in that there was a big mirror and a noticeboard and a small table with a huge bunch of white lilies in the middle, which smelt lovely, almost lovely enough to counteract the very strong odour of feet.

Kurt was tuning his guitar when I went in, and he looked up with this great big smile, which, as he clocked who it was, fell off his face and smashed into pieces all over the floor.

'Hi!' I said.

'*You?*'

He didn't look especially overjoyed that I was there.

In fact, I'd go as far as to say that I was the person he least wanted to see in the entire universe.

'Yes, me.'

'Get out.'

'Um . . .'

'Go!'

I didn't – couldn't – move, and that just made him shout louder.

'I've supported you from the beginning. Right back

when you did your first single and stupid Tony wouldn't release it, I defended you. And I let you put out a song where you basically accused my music, my *art*, of being worthless.'

I crumpled as the words hit me.

'I was nice to you. I respected you, even after you dragged me into the stupid Karamel vs Katie fight, which I never wanted because I liked your music. I liked *you*. And you still thought I'd sell you out to Pop Trash, and not only that, you went public and told everyone?! What does that make me look like?' He spun a small, angry circle. 'And why are you still here?'

'Because . . . I've come to take it all back. OK? I'm a complete idiot and you don't have to forgive me.'

'I wasn't planning to.'

Once again, I was coming to realize the importance of making a plan before you get into the room with someone important.

Only, really, what else could I say? Other than:

'I'm sorry. I'm sorry for all of it. For the song, the rubbish pathetic excuse for a song, which I only wrote to get back at my best friend for ignoring me on my birthday.'

He didn't look any happier. He certainly didn't look like the apology was helping. But he hadn't chucked me out. So:

'And the chart battle, which was low. And pointless. Who cares if some people like one thing and some people like another? There's room in the world for all of us. More than that, though, I should never have let it carry on, after the concert, when I realized you were good.'

'No. You shouldn't have.'

I managed to look up and meet his eyes, his huge, beautiful eyes the colour of new conkers, and saw that he hated me, so much.

'I did everything wrong.'

'You did.'

'And it turns out it was my dad who sold the story on me if you can imagine how that feels, and Adrian's committed to spending six hundred pounds on Savannah for getting me in here, so you don't have to listen to my apology but I do at least have to stand in front of you and say it.'

'What the . . . ?'

'I know! But I promised her a Gucci bag. I maybe

should have checked the cost first, but there we go.'

'I meant, the story came from your *dad*?'

'Um. Yeah.' I'd promised myself I wouldn't cry, and I very nearly kept it.

'That's harsh.'

'He didn't know what he was doing,' I said quickly. Then, 'Which, really, is just as bad as if he did.'

'I'd had it down as being a teacher or someone your mum works with. Or a mate. Well, a so-called mate.'

'He's a so-called dad,' I said. 'I should've known. I've been so stupid.'

I caught a glimpse of myself in that big mirror and looked away. I'm sure that mirror has seen lots of interesting things, being situated in the main dressing room at Wembley Arena. Still, I bet it has never seen anyone produce such a spectacular quantity of snot as me.

Nor, by his expression, had Kurt. Even so, he came and sat next to me, and I saw that something in what I'd said had pierced him, somehow. 'It's not stupid to love someone. It's not stupid to trust your father.'

'No?'

'It's not stupid to have faith in people. Even if they let you down. You keep having faith in them. Maybe they'll live up to it.' He smiled that amazing smile. 'That's what I tell myself about *my* dad. It hasn't worked so far. But you never know.'

I looked at my feet. 'I don't think I have much faith in me, any more.'

'Um, quick question – because I do want to talk about this, but we're supposed to be onstage fairly soon – where is Kolin?'

'Oh. Yes. Um, Kolin's with Savannah. They're getting back together.' I thought about exactly what this might entail. 'You might want to text him.'

He did, and I watched his face frowning over his phone. Not in a weird, stalkery way or anything.

OK, in a slightly stalkery way. But I don't think it counts as stalking if the person finishes texting and looks up at you and grins.

Which made me blush so much that I looked away, and made myself stare very hard at a bit of paper stuck to the noticeboard.

A running order. Which went like this:

TEEN TIME AWARDS

Olly Murs

Ed Sheeran

Tinie Tempah

Little Mix

Bruno Mars

~~Katie Cox~~

Rita Ora

Karamel

'What's my name doing up there?'

'I thought you'd won something,' said Kurt.

'I don't think so.'

'You must have done.'

'No. Except, maybe . . .' My mind rewound to that conversation with Tony, on an afternoon where everything had still seemed possible. 'I did win something, I think. But that was before . . . everything . . .'

'You could still sing, you know,' said Kurt, in this light voice that completely went against the enormous weight of what he was suggesting.

'Um, ha ha – I don't think so.'

'Why not?'

'You want reasons? OK. For one thing, literally the entire stadium wants me to be erased from the face of the earth. So there's that. Also, I don't have my guitar with me. Also, I'm done with music.'

'Katie, you can't give up music.'

'Watch me.' Not that there was anything to actually watch, but, you know.

'You're never going to play again?'

'I made some rules, if you must know. I can't play or sing anything unless I hum something without realizing, and I'm allowed to sing if it would be weird not to, like, say, I'm at a party and someone brings in a birthday cake. And—'

'You're happy with this? As a decision? For the rest of your life?'

And I wanted to scream at him. That, no, of course I wasn't happy with it. That I was basically trapping myself in a grey, soulless universe of nothingness, as though all the flavour had been drained from everything that mattered, like when you eat a strawberry in February, only multiplied by everything, for always and ever.

'I just . . . don't want to make things any worse.'

'I guess.' He nodded. 'Yeah. It's sad, but . . . it makes sense.'

'Yeah.'

So, that was it, then. I'd made my apology.

Everything was finished.

I should go home.

Maybe start looking for a Gucci flash sale or something.

Then a voice made me look up. A sweet, tender voice. Singing a familiar tune.

Quite like guitar girl
And I do have a tattoo

Kurt was strumming on his guitar.

Quite like guitar girl
Thinking she should get one too

Then he stopped. 'Mine's not Chinese, FYI.' He rolled up a sleeve to reveal golden skin and something complicated going on just above his elbow. 'It's Celtic. I had it done on tour. In Latvia, of all places.'

'Cool.'

'Not really. My mum went berserk. Technically, I think I'm still grounded.'

I found myself smiling. Just a bit. 'OK, I'll update it.' I lifted the guitar across and into my arms.

> The tattooed Celtic symbol
> On skin that's nicely tanned

'Better?'

'Better,' said Kurt. 'Anything else you want to change?'

We were very close as I sang.

> Quite like the boy band
> Their upbeat melodies
> Quite like the boy band
> Kinda pop-py kinda cheese
>
> It's cool they love their grannies
> And their devoted fans
> I quite like the boy band

'Only *quite*?' said Kurt.

'More than quite,' I said, looking away.

I like the boy band
It's a different way to be
I like the boy band
Their vibe is so happy
And if there's a chance they'll take it
Then I'll offer them my hand
Yes, I like the boy band.

I finished and he took my hand from the strings and held it in his.

It was an amazing moment.

Which I ruined, by blurting out:

'Look. I've said my thing. I should let you get on. With singing to all of Wembley.'

'Ed's just come off stage. We've still got time,' said Kurt. Then, seeing my confusion, 'Ed Sheeran. He's really nice.'

'Oh good,' I said. 'I'd hate it if he wasn't.'

We both looked at the wall, and at my name, crossed out.

And . . . it's hard to explain how I could feel so sure of it, but I knew, I just knew, that we'd both had the same thought.

'You should—'

'I can't—'

It was so big and so terrible that I couldn't even begin to put it into words.

'Kurt, I *can't*.'

'Katie, you can.'

'But . . . I'm giving up music.'

He didn't say anything.

'Everyone hates me.'

He still didn't say anything. The messages from Tony's computer screen scrolled invisibly between us. So much hate. Out there. So close. And all of it for me.

'Kurt, it's not . . . I can't.'

His eyes were so gentle, this luscious, delicious brown. Like chocolate mousse. Only then, they frosted over. Like chocolate mousse that's been stuck right at the back of the fridge.

'All right. I thought you were truly sorry. But . . .'

'I am!'

'Then show me.'

'You want me to sing.'

'I do.'

'You want me to sing "Can't Stand the Boy Band"? To all of Wembley?'

 331

'I do. I'll even lend you my guitar.'

'Wow. Wait. No. Maybe. I mean, I could sing "Cake Boyfriend". Or "Spaghetti Hoops" – no, not that – but I could definitely do "Leftover Chinese Takeaway Blues". It's got a real swing to it . . .'

Even as I said it, I knew. If I was going to get up there, I had to sing 'Can't Stand the Boy Band'. Anything else would be a massive cop-out.

'I can't do it.'

At which point, Jaz came bursting through the door and went:

'Ha ha ha, you're Kurt from Karamel, ha ha ha.'

'Jaz!'

She was followed by Savannah and Kolin, whose face was covered in Savanna's lipgloss, and Kristian, and Adrian, and Lacey, who twiddled her hair and said, 'Hi I love your music sorry just ignore me.'

'Please,' said Jaz, as my BF stared at the floor. 'Hold it together.'

'This is Kurt from Karamel!' wailed Lacey.

'And you're Lacey from Harltree.' She looked up, and I was just thinking that maybe this was the moment when they might actually become friends, when Jaz followed it up with, 'Lacey Daniels, you are slightly less pathetic than you think you are.'

Lace made a face.

Jaz made a face.

Kurt was laughing.

And I thought, this will do, actually. Just, everyone together, they don't have to be the besties or anything. They can take the mick out of each other, if they have to. Just . . .

Oh. My. God.

OH MY GOD.

'I know how to do this,' I said. 'I'm going to do it. I'm going to sing.'

'There we go,' said Kurt.

'Why?' said Kolin, who was still looking at Savannah.

'You are going to get minced,' said Lacey.

CHAPTER THIRTY-ONE

So there I was, standing in the wings, ready to do my first major concert. I mean, seriously major, with masses of people watching and goodness knows how many more online.

Even though I'd practised and practised, I was shaking so badly I could barely hold my guitar. My hands were dripping sweat, and there was a fair chance that when I opened my mouth I'd barf all over the stage.

It was no use telling myself that everyone gets nervous. Because this was no ordinary concert.

I was about to sing live to twelve and a half thousand people.

And each and every one of them wanted to kill me.

In fact, it's less complicated than you'd think, getting on the bill of the Teen Time Awards at Wembley Arena. I mean, it helps if you were on it originally before you got yourself struck off by being dropped from your record label.

Plus, it's an advantage if you've got the lead singer of a monstrously famous boy band to talk to the high-up people and convince them that it's a good idea. Backed by your amazing manager, Adrian.

Also, Bruno Mars was stuck in America because his flight had been cancelled and the show was going to be way too short.

So, in the space of approximately ten minutes, I'd gone from being a slightly carsick nobody, wearing my sloppiest tracksuit bottoms, with my hair completely everywhere and a breakout so bad that I looked like I was having some kind of allergic reaction, to . . .

Entirely the same person, only holding Kurt's guitar.

'She cannot go onstage like that,' Savannah was saying. 'It's like, if you're going to die, you should at least be a beautiful corpse.'

'Thanks, Savannah, that's really helpful.'

'I . . . I've got some concealer. It's not much. And it's the wrong shade. But . . .'

The words came from a very unexpected source.

'Lace . . . are you sure?'

'You know you can catch spots from sharing make-up, don't you?' said Savannah.

'I know,' said Lacey.

'You don't have to,' I said.

She leaned in to dot and then smear concealer on to my forehead, and I got a close-up of the inside of her mouth as she said, 'What you said. In the car. You *were* a bad friend to me. But, I wasn't there for you. On your birthday. And . . . you're going to get pulled apart out there. If this is the last time I see you, I'd rather we said goodbye as friends.'

'So . . .' I didn't know what to say. 'Am I allowed to wear my charm bracelet, then?'

'If you like,' said Lacey.

'I do like,' I said, and maybe we'd have hugged, or maybe we wouldn't, as she still looked a bit wary. I've got no way of knowing because just then, a man with a clipboard knocked, in that brisk way that means someone's going to come in whether you're sharing an emotional moment or not, and came in.

'Katie Cox? Tech team. So it's just you, a mic and an acoustic guitar?'

'Yeah,' I said.

'Nothing for us to project behind you? Everyone else has a video, or lights, or something.'

'No,' I said. 'Sorry.'

'Hey, can I have your phone?' said Jaz.

'Why?'

'Can't tell you now,' said Jaz. 'But trust me, OK?'

Just to recap. The first time Jaz had held a phone in my presence, she'd put me on to the internet and simultaneously made and destroyed my entire life. The next time I lent her my phone, she'd nearly given my mother a heart attack. So you can see why I wasn't ever so keen.

Which I suppose is why she just leaned over and grabbed it out of my hand.

'Jaz! Jaz, come back. JAZ!'

Clipboard man tapped his clipboard. 'If you'd like to follow me upstairs, Katie? You're next.'

Up we went. Up and round and along the bright corridors, in this kind of procession of doom, and then suddenly, we could hear them, the crowd, just ahead. Not the noise I'd heard back at my little concert. Not even the shrieking at the Karamel gig.

This was like . . . the sea. A proper sea, an ocean, a swell of sound that went back and back.

'Catch her, she's going down.'

'No, no, I'm OK, it's all right,' I said. 'It's not even that many people, really. Is it?'

We'd reached the wings, and I looked out.

And it was huge. Epic. A city of people, of twinkling phones and glowsticks, neatly stacked in blocks that went on and on and on and up and up.

'Good luck, Katie.'

'Good luck.'

'Good luck.'

'RIP, babes.' That one was Savannah.

'Now, the winner of the Teen Time People's Award. Bit of a controversial one, this award was decided before recent . . . events. But, she's here now, with her new song. It's KATIE COX!'

I don't know if you've ever heard twelve and a half thousand people gasp all at the same time.

It's quite something.

Then, silence.

My legs were carrying me out into the light.

Down, on to the little stool they'd put there.

Fingers, shaking, into place on the guitar, as the first boos began.

A chord.

The wrong chord.
Stop.
Take a breath.
More boos. Louder now.
Then . . .

 Quite like the boy band

A wave of jeering.

Their upbeat melodies

Keep going, Katie.

Quite like the boy band
Kinda pop-py kinda cheese

It's cool they love their grannies
And their devoted fans
I quite like the boy band

And then – they cheered!
Not loudly. And not for long. But they did.

Quite like the boy band
It's a different way to be
Quite like the boy band
Their vibe is so happy

Another cheer. Big enough to drown out the boos, which were still coming. I felt my voice lift, as though I'd stepped from a boat on to solid ground.

And if there's a chance they'll take it
Then I'll offer them my hand
Yes, I like the boy band

Something was happening. The glowing phones, which had been waving in all different directions . . . they were all waving . . . together.

I went into the instrumental section, which was quite tricky, and so maybe that's why the crowd noticed before I did . . . and it was only as I heard this infinite screaming roar that I realized . . .

Kurt was next to me.

And he sang:

Quite like guitar girl
And I do have a tattoo
Quite like guitar girl
Thinking she should get one too

Her lyrics make me chuckle
But her bedroom makes me hurl
Yeah, I quite like guitar girl

And something made me glance back, up, behind us . . .

I don't know how Jaz had done it.

But there was my face, singing in my bedroom. Then Karamel, sitting in their camper van. Then, the messages, from me to Kurt, from Kurt back to me. And the comments, all of them, the love and the hate, flashing faster and faster and faster . . .

And we sang:

Let's make a new band
While the music's feeling right
Let's start a new band
Singing out into the night

341

Yes if there's a chance you'll take it
Then I'm giving you my hand
You and me, a new band

Kurt was clapping, and I held out the mic, like I'd only ever seen on TV, the charms on my bracelet flashing under spotlights hotter than the sun.

'Sing with me, Wembley':

And if there's a chance you'll take it
Then I'm giving you my hand
Just tonight; a new band.

They sang in a way I couldn't just hear, but feel. They sang it over and over and over again.

In the wings, Savannah and Adrian were singing.

And Lacey was singing.

And even, blimey – even Jaz.

When Vernon Kay came bounding on to the stage and said, 'Give it up for Katie Cox, winner of the Teen Time New Act Award!' I kind of hardly noticed.

The applause began, and I lifted my arms.

'Peace and love,' said Kurt. 'Peace and love.'

A microphone was shoved into my face. 'Katie?'

'Peace and love,' I said.

And then cracked up, because, I mean, *honestly*.

CHAPTER THIRTY-TWO

Afterwards, everything went berserk.

My plan had been to hide in the dressing room, or perhaps get back into the car and go home, but instead we got swept along by the clipboard people into this gigantic room, which pulsed and throbbed with lights and music and was completely packed with people wearing special wristbands and very little else, all drinking champagne like they were dying of thirst or something.

'Bruno's going crazy that he missed it. Heads will roll.'

and

'They didn't do that at the soundcheck.'

and

'Are those two an item? There's definitely something going on there.'

I kind of shuffled in, still horribly aware that I had my tracksuit on and only the very minimum of make-up, and stood in the corner trying not to look at anyone.

Which was quite difficult, as everyone – and I mean *everyone* – wanted to look at me.

I had pretty much the whole of the iTunes top 100 come up and congratulate me, which was nice although deeply embarrassing, and once Jaz had given me my phone back I got some cool selfies, which was even nicer, but nicest of all was the Appletiser that Lace brought over. In the end, Lacey, Jaz and Adrian had to form a protective circle so that I could drink it.

Which was an OK way of spending the party, pointing and laughing at the various bonkers outfits everyone had turned up in, until Adrian stepped back to say:

'Katie. It's Tony.'

At the exact same time, my phone started going.

'Sorry,' I said. 'Important phone call . . . Oh . . .' It was Dad. I hit reject, then looked up to do the same to my ex-label boss.

He was right in front of me, his teeth glowing in the ultraviolet light. Or maybe there wasn't any ultraviolet, maybe they were just glowing anyway. Maybe they weren't even teeth, just two rows of tooth-shaped light bulbs.

'Look –' I began, not really knowing where I was going with this, but feeling like I needed to say something.

'I know.'

345

'It's just . . .' I hid my face in my glass.

'I'll say it, shall I? We shouldn't have dropped you so fast.'

'I understand why you did.' Which was true. 'I'd have done the same, if I were you.'

'Be that as it may, I was actually coming over to suggest you join another label. There's a job for your dad whatever you do, of course, but we're assuming you'll want to go elsewhere.'

What?

'Oh. Right.' My brain finally caught up with the conversation. 'And actually, you were the one who set up the whole Karamel-rivalry-single-release-on-the-same-day thing. So, you shouldn't have dropped me so fast!'

'No,' he said.

'I should join another label?!'

'You should. We're too easily scared by bad press. We'd never had a situation like that, and we panicked. It was irresponsible and it was unkind. It won't happen again, but of course you'll want to go elsewhere. I'm thinking Monumental Beats would be a good place for you; I'll get you a meeting with Scarlett. Or there's FRD, Bethany's a peach . . .'

'I don't need another label,' I said. 'I'm not doing music any more. I'm going back to being normal.'

'Katie.' He stood next to me and we looked out over the room. The woman nearest us was wearing a top open almost to the waist. She lifted her arm to wave, and flashed me. 'You can't go back to normal, Katie. You've gone too far for that.'

'I haven't, it's only been a few weeks, but it'll happen.' I tried not to think about that hideous night at the Harvester. 'It might be a while, but I will.'

'Your song. Just now. It's the number one trending topic worldwide.'

'Look, Tony, no one says "trending topic", just like no one says "social media" and . . .' I digested what he'd just told me. 'Come again?'

'Your performance just now is the number one trending topic on the planet.'

'I don't . . .'

'People are saying you've brought whole worlds of music together. You've become this symbol of reconciliation. Of friendship.'

'In the last half-hour?!'

'Doesn't take long.'

'They'll forget. Everyone will forget.'

'If that's what you want.'

Then Jessie J came over. In real life her hair looks even better than it does on TV, super glossy and perfectly straight.

Eventually she went off to talk to Emeli Sandé, and Tony turned back to me with a sad smile.

'Is there anything I can say? You're a marvel, Katie. You have the world at your feet. That, there, tonight – *that's* your single. The live recording. I've already had calls from about nine different countries. We'll put it on the album with "Just Me", "Cake Boyfriend", "Autocorrect" – maybe not the one about spaghetti hoops . . . but otherwise, you can choose. We won't interfere. And then . . . your summer holidays are coming up, aren't they? How would you like to come with us to the States? The UK – that's great, that's all well and good, but we need to be thinking globally now. We'll fly you first class; you can bring a friend, if you want. Two friends. We'll put you up somewhere fancy, get you the best of everything. All you need to do is sing like you did tonight.'

'I can't. I made the decision. That was my last song.'

He sighed. 'Look. Katie. I know I'm the villain. But just

tell me this. Has anyone, *anyone*, heard your plan to give up music and told you that it's a good idea?'

I didn't want to have to shake my head.

And, as it turned out, I didn't have to.

'You know where to find me,' said Tony. 'Whether you want to stay with Top Music, sign with a new label, whatever. Like it or not, you're a star now.'

I spent a few minutes gazing out into that crowded room, and thinking how incredibly upsetting it was that I didn't feel like I fitted in here any more than I did at school, and really, was there not a single party in the world where a girl could have a good time?!

Then I took my phone on to the balcony to tell the one person who definitely would approve of my decision.

'Hi, Mum.'

'Katie. I am going to kill you. Honestly. The second I get my hands on you . . . I am going to . . . I'm . . . so . . . I'm so . . .'

'Mum, are you *crying*?'

'I'm so proud of you.'

'Oh. OK.'

'The last few days have been appalling. Then I get a message from Ade, we put the telly on, me and your father. One minute we're in front of *Coronation Street*, the next, we're watching our little girl lighting up London.'

'Well . . .'

'And, I don't like it. I don't.'

'I know.'

'But I see now, you've got to do this, haven't you?'

Now I was crying, a bit. 'I don't know if I can. What you said, about not getting hurt. I'm going to get hurt, aren't I?'

'Yes. But . . . you'll get hurt anyway. Whatever you do. I can't protect you forever.'

'I don't think I'm strong enough.'

'I know you are, Katie.'

'Mum . . .' I let the pause sit between us for a while, because it seemed to say what I wanted to better than words. Then, 'Mum, it was Dad. He was the one who sold the story.'

'He told me.'

'I'll never forgive him.'

A snort. 'It's hardly the worst thing he's ever done.'

'I kn-know. He's been . . . he shouldn't have . . . Ending it with you and then running off to America with Catriona and blowing all that money and then . . . I get it now.

And I'm never going to speak to him again. I promise you that.'

'Katie, your father is a total idiot. A complete and utter . . .' She stopped herself. 'But of course you'll speak to him again. He's your dad. He loves you. And . . . it's hard for him, being the brilliant, talented idiot that he is and having to live with himself.'

'So?'

'So . . . when you were onstage tonight, I saw him. In you.'

'No!'

'He's a part of you,' said Mum. 'He knows he did the wrong thing. He understands that.'

Since when did Mum stand up for Dad?

'He's here. Next to me. He wants to say sorry. I do think he means it. Will you speak to him, Katie?'

'Not now,' I said. 'Maybe, later.' I wiped my eyes. 'Is Mands around?'

'Hold on, she's just come through the door. AMANDA? YOUR SISTER WANTS TO TALK TO YOU.'

'How was the gig? Was the shop full? Did people come?' I was gabbling.

'What about *you*?! I've just been reading about

everything on my phone. You are nuts, you know that? Totally nuts . . . Katie? Katie, what's wrong?'

'Dad,' I said. 'I've just . . . Mum said . . .' I tried to pull myself together. 'I can't forgive him. Can I? I don't think I can.'

'I'm trying,' said Mands.

'He'll go back to America soon,' I said. 'He's got a job waiting for him.'

'Maybe you'll find it easier that way,' said Amanda, so gently that it made my eyelids prickle.

Which I wanted to believe. I really did.

He's so proud of you, Catriona had said. *He loves you so much.*

Then, I knew.

That if I let him go, I'd be letting go of a part of myself. Someone who, yes, was totally and completely selfish. Then again, I hadn't been much better lately.

And to forgive people, to love people, you have to be there.

Oh, Dad.

As I made the decision, then and there, Lacey appeared on one side of me, and Jaz on the other.

'Lacey was worrying about you,' said Jaz. 'I said she's

probably off doing shots with someone from the telly.'

'Which would be very worrying,' said Lacey. She peered at me. '*Have* you been doing shots? You look awful. Talk to me, Katie. Talk to me!'

What I wanted to say was that I'd never really meant to bring the world back together.

But then, I'd not especially meant to tear it apart.

'Urgh! That is revolting.'

We looked down to see Savannah and Kolin kissing underneath a whole bunch of fairy lights. Savannah had her phone out, and was simultaneously taking a selfie.

'So, is Kurt going to be your boyfriend?' said Lacey.

'Er, no. I am not the sort of person who goes out with someone in a boy band, thank you very much.'

'Aren't you? Because when you two were onstage . . . it looked like . . . you might . . .'

'No way!' I caught myself. 'Well, I dunno. He'd have to ditch the fake tan and all those hairstyles. But, he's a decent enough guitarist.'

'Not to mention incredibly good-looking and an amazing singer and, um, the most desirable boy on the planet.'

'Yeah,' I said, going very red indeed. 'Even so, though,

I'm not exactly going to take him to the school disco, am I?'

'Probably not,' said Lacey. 'Given that it was tonight. I guess if we got in the car right now . . . we'd catch the bit where everyone leaves and goes home.'

'What?' This was not good. 'You missed it? For this? Lacey, I owe you. Big time.'

'S'OK. Wouldn't have been much fun without you, anyway.'

'You're a good friend, Lacey Daniels.'

'And you, Katie Cox, are a rubbish one. It's lucky you can get me into such cool parties, really.'

'The best friend ever,' I said.

'Ahem.'

'And so are you, Jasmine James. Although I don't remember giving you permission to go broadcasting the contents of my phone to the whole of Wembley Arena.'

'Like I need your permission,' murmured Jaz.

We stood there, the three of us, and watched the party.

'So . . . are you doing anything good this summer?'

'Mum was talking about us going to Tenerife but she hasn't booked yet as she says the best deals are always last minute. But she said that last year and then she couldn't get one, so we ended up in Monmouth.'

Jaz said, 'Why?'

'I was thinking,' I said. 'How would you like to come with me to America?'

Lacey began to scream so loudly that I didn't hear Jaz's reply.

And she carried on screaming, and maybe I did too, down the stairs, and back into the car, with Adrian and (a reluctant) Savannah, all the way back to Harltree.

The lights whizzed past on the motorway, Beyoncé came through loud on the stereo, and Adrian rolled down the windows so that the warm night could flow over us.

Lacey was teaching Jaz this special dance you can do sitting down, Beyoncé was Beyoncé, her voice flying like rockets, while Savannah was compiling a complicated order of beauty products that apparently you can only get stateside.

And all while this was happening, a bit of me was thinking about Dad, and whether he'd have time to hang out between doing whatever work Tony was finding for him. Another bit of me was googling my name, and then having to stop because it seemed like the rest of the internet had been pretty much put on hold to make way for stuff about Katie Cox.

Most of me, though, was laughing and singing and doing fancy footwork in the back of that car.

I didn't know whether I was making the right decision.

Maybe no one ever does.

But I wasn't saying goodbye to music. Not now, not any time soon.

Whatever it meant, wherever it led.

And that, at least, felt right.

THE END

ABOUT THE AUTHOR

Marianne Levy spent her twenties as an actor. She was in various TV shows, did some comedy on Radio 4 and made a brief appearance in the film *Ali G Indahouse*, where she managed to forget both her lines. She then worked as a continuity announcer for Living TV, introducing, and getting obsessed with, *America's Next Top Model*. She's been the voice of a leading brand of make-up, a shopping centre and a yogurt. Marianne has written for the *Independent*, the *Independent on Sunday*, *How to Spend It*, the *Guardian* and the *i*. She lives in London with her husband, daughter and a bad-tempered cat.

www.mariannelevy.com

Find out how Katie Cox's story began in . . .

IF I'D KNOWN THAT TWO MILLION PEOPLE
WERE GOING TO BE WATCHING, I'D PROBABLY
HAVE DONE A BIT OF TIDYING UP.

Katie Cox is used to going unnoticed — by her mum, her dad,
even her best friend. But when a video of her singing in her
bedroom goes viral, she becomes a superstar overnight.
As the views skyrocket and a recording contract beckons,
the real world starts to feel very far away.

And now Katie's riding high on her new-found fame.
But the higher she goes, the further there is to fall . . .

OUT NOW!